the magic of grace

The Magic of
Grace

Rick Machamer

The Magic of Grace
© 2012 by Rick Machamer

All rights reserved. This book or any portion thereof may not be reproduced or used in any manner whatsoever without the express written permission of the publishers except for the use of brief quotations in a book review.

Unless otherwise noted, all Scripture quotations are taken from the *Holy Bible, New International Version®,* NIV®. Copyright © 1973, 1978, 1984, 2011 by Biblica, Inc. Used by permission of Zondervan. All rights reserved.

Scripture quotations marked LB are from *The Living Bible*. Copyright © 1971 owned by assignment by KNT Charitable Trust.

Published by
Deep River Books
Sisters, Oregon
www.deepriverbooks.com

ISBN–13: 9781937756499
ISBN–10: 1937756491

Library of Congress: 2012948892

Printed in the USA

Cover design by Becky Barbier

CONTENTS

    Prologue 7

1   The Bookstore and the Magician 17
    Prevenient Grace

2   Camp Sequoyah 27

3   A Second Chance 39
    Abundant Grace

4   The Scoutmaster 47

5   On the Way Back from Breakfast 53
    You Are Not Alone

6   Night Attack 67

7   The Canvas Sanctuary 77

8   Drew's First Magic Show and
   Mr. Michaels's Final Bow 81

    Epilogue 93

ACKNOWLEDGMENTS

When I was young, my father would entertain us kids by performing magic tricks. Over time, he collected quite an assortment of trick card decks and magic boxes, along with a fake bunny rabbit, which kept us captivated for hours.

For many years, I played with the idea of writing a story about a boy who crossed paths with an unusual old man who does magic. The magician used his gift of conjuring not for profit, but to instill in the boy the confidence and courage to overcome adversity and challenges. You will find some of my dad in this story.

I tinkered with it a long time, until one day, finally, it came to me in a powerful way how I should go about telling this story. For that, I must thank the team members of the Virginia Peninsula Rainbow Emmaus Community. They explained to me the many means of God's grace at a time when I especially needed it. They probably won't remember the words I nervously spoke at the closing of my walk to Emmaus. But I do: "For what God has done for me during the past days, I will give something back." This story, my Emmaus brothers and sister, is my fourth day.

And to Adam Blumer, editor extraordinaire: Every writer, no matter how good he or she *thinks* they are, needs an editor. I can't thank Adam enough. Not only did he edit my text, but he took the time, and I'm sure sometimes painful effort, to teach me new things about style and presentation. If you enjoy reading this story, you can thank him more than me.

Finally, the inspiration for this work came not from me. Before He returned to Heaven, Jesus told his disciples to feed His sheep; to carry His word to all creation. In a small way, *The Magic of Grace* is in obedience to the command He gave all of us.

PROLOGUE

The stage was aglow with sparks that hovered about like fireflies.

The yellow-orange light from the huge bonfire behind the stage accentuated the magician's aura. His shadow mysteriously followed his every move as he performed his illusions.

The bonfire supplied most of the lighting for the show, and later it would provide the venue for roasting marshmallows and telling ghost stories.

Just after sunset the scoutmaster had introduced Mr. Drew Seward to the thirty Cub Scouts on an overnight camping trip. He was The Magic Man, the star attraction for tonight's entertainment.

Bobby sat on the grass directly in front of the stage. He was mesmerized as he followed the magician's every move. After watching a cane burst into a colorful flower bouquet quicker than the blink of an eye, Bobby turned to the magician's son, sitting cross-legged next to him.

"Danny, how does your Dad do this stuff? What's the secret?"

"Don't worry about it," Danny said. "Just watch the show."

Bobby looked at another kid behind him. "Did you see how he did that?"

"Nope."

He turned his attention back to the stage. *OK. He's not going to fool me this time. I'm gonna watch real close.*

"For my next trick, boys, I refer you to the magic box," the magician said. He pointed to a red wooden container sitting on the table next to him.

Bobby studied it, looking for anything suspicious. About the size of a shoebox, it was trimmed with gold fringe and decorated with elaborate, yellow Chinese markings.

The magician unlatched the side of the box and opened it to

face the crowd. The box was empty. To prove "there is nothing there," he took his magic wand and moved it freely back and forth inside the vacant space.

Bobby was a little skeptical, but…*OK, it's gotta be empty. I think.*

The Magic Man closed the magic box and picked it up, turning it so the boys could see all six sides. He rapped each side with his fist to show the box was indeed solid. He placed it back down on the table and opened the top.

The magician reached in and pulled out a wiggling bundle of white fur.

Bobby shook his head. *Wow! Where'd the rabbit come from?*

"Well, wadda ya know," the magician said. "Look what I found."

He carried the rabbit to the front of the stage.

"Boys, this is my friend, Herby," the magician said, cradling the rabbit in his hands. The boys cheered and clapped for Herby. The bunny wiggled, trying to escape.

"If I was Herby," Bobby said to Danny, "I'd be squirming, too. Get me outta here." He laughed.

Bobby was now more fascinated with the rabbit than with where it had mysteriously come from. Bobby once had a rabbit his parents gave him at Easter. He used to love playing with his rabbit before it ran away. Maybe Mr. Seward would let him play with Herby after the show.

The magician gently gripped Herby's front paw. Herby waved to the audience. "Say good-bye to the nice boys, Herby. It's time to go to bed."

He returned to the table and gently lowered the rabbit back into the box, closed the lid, and latched it shut.

"Well, that's the show for this evening," the magician said. "I hope you enjoyed it." He removed his black top hat and took a bow. "So good night, boys. It's time for me to go to bed as well."

The Scouts watched in silence as he waved, walked off stage right, and disappeared.

Bobby whispered to Danny, "What's up, man? Is that it?"

I didn't get a chance to hold the rabbit.

Danny just grinned and shrugged.

Bobby persisted. "So, what are we gonna do now? Where are we supposed to go?"

"Just shut up and hold on for a minute."

Hold on for what?

Other than the wood popping in the fire, the outdoor auditorium was strangely quiet.

Suddenly creepy laughter drifted from somewhere behind them: a fairy-tale witch sort of laugh. Evil and nasty.

Their heads turned.

A fiendish character stomped down the hill toward the stage. The boys in its path scooted aside as if to avoid being trampled. Bobby leaned over to hide behind Danny.

The ghoul wore a black robe. His matching cape with the bloodred lining fanned out as he stepped through the crowd.

"Out of my way, you little urchins!" he yelled. "I'm late for supper!"

His jet-black hair was long and stringy. His face was grotesque: all green and distorted and covered with big, ugly moles. His long, pointed nose almost reached his lower lip.

Peeking around Danny, Bobby caught the reflection of something long and shiny in the monster's hand.

"Watch out!" he yelled when he realized…"He's got a knife!"

But before anyone could react, whatever it was jumped onto the stage and slowly crept toward the box, brandishing a long, thin dagger above his head.

Bobby watched, wide-eyed and scared, as the ghoul glared at them. He snarled. "Herby is somewhat in a bit of trouble now, don't you think?" He grabbed his stomach and bellowed that wicked "hee hee hee" laugh again. He lifted the box with his left hand and wielded the dagger in his right.

Bobby sensed something sinister was about to happen. *He wouldn't really hurt Herby. Would he? Please don't kill Herby.*

One boy shouted, "Let Herby go!"

But the monster was unswayed. "I am Mr. McEvel!" he cried. "And I'm hungry for rabbit stew!" He twirled the knife and lined it up with one of the fabricated holes cut into the side of the box. Bobby feared the box would soon be Herby's coffin.

This has to be a joke, Bobby thought. *It can't be real. He wouldn't really do that…would he?*

Danny was smiling.

"What's so funny, Danny?" he whispered. "He's getting ready to kill the rabbit."

Suddenly, a haunting laugh came from the stage. Bobby looked up and watched in horror as the monster thrust the blade into the hole. Again and again. Three or four times. Bobby yelled and groaned with every thrust, as did the rest of the audience.

The mean demon-thing had skewered poor Herby.

I hope they nab you so I can punch you in the face. I'll show you, you jerk.

Finished with the dastardly deed, Mr. McEvel withdrew the weapon and laid it aside. Still holding the box in the air, he snickered and said, "Ohhh, this could be messy." With his free hand, he unhooked the latch.

Bobby covered his eyes. Blood made him squeamish.

The side facing the crowd fell open.

"Bobby, look!" Danny said.

The box was empty.

Bobby sighed.

Thank goodness. Herby must have escaped.

Mr. McEvel looked inside. He felt all around the inside. Nothing but air. He shook his head; he looked somewhat confused.

He closed the box and set it down on the table. Suddenly, he whirled around. Looking up, he raised his fists into the air and let off a loud roar.

"What happened to my dinner?" Mr. McEvel yelled. He grabbed the dagger and rushed to the front of the stage. He

THE MAGIC OF GRACE

pointed the knife at the closet boy in the front row. Who happened to be Bobby.

"Did you steal my supper, little boy?"

Bobby stared at the monster as he edged closer with the knife. He wanted to run, but fear froze him in place. He felt his heart beating in his chest.

"Leave my friend alone, you ole bones," Danny yelled.

Bobby glanced at Danny. Why was he still laughing?

The ghoul stopped. His hand holding the knife dropped to his side.

He grabbed his chin and pulled the mask from his face.

Bobby stared. *What?*

It was Mr. Seward. He had returned.

Mr. Seward smiled. And the boys breathed a collective sigh of relief.

Especially Bobby.

He shook his head and sighed.

It was just a trick.

"Bobby, you did a great job," Mr. Seward said, smiling at him.

Bobby wasn't sure what he'd done, but he sure was glad to see Danny's father back.

Mr. Seward, the magician, turned around and went back to the table.

"OK, boys. We'd better check on Herby." He opened the lid, reached in, and pulled out the rabbit, holding it by the back of the neck.

Bobby relaxed. It was over. Herby was unscathed, very much alive and well.

Cradling the rabbit, Mr. Seward presented it to the audience. "Here he is. All safe and sound!"

The boys clapped and cheered. An assistant pack leader trotted onstage right on cue. The magician handed Herby over to him, and the rabbit was quickly whisked away.

The magical portion of the show was over. The magician took his final bow. The Scouts clapped and whistled. They wanted more magic. Instead, Mr. Seward smiled and held up two fingers, the Cub Scout sign to get their attention.

The boys settled down, and the noise dwindled as Mr. Seward picked up a Bible from the table where he kept his props.

"Thanks, guys. I hope you enjoyed the show and had fun," he said. "But here's what I want you to remember. What I did tonight, and what you saw here, were just tricks. They're not real."

He held up the Bible. "But God doesn't do tricks. God performs miracles. And His miracles are real."

He opened the Bible and turned to the book of Job. "I want to tell you a story about this man named Job. Most of you have heard of him."

Bobby knew about Job. *Yeah, I remember him from Sunday school. There's a picture of him in my Bible, sitting in a pile of ashes and dirt. The Devil put a curse on him, or somethin' like that.*

"Many bad things happened to Job that were out of his control," Mr. Seward said. "His entire family was killed in a tornado. All his farm animals were slaughtered or stolen by rustlers. All his workers were killed. He contracted a disease that caused sores to break out all over his body. Everything bad that could happen to someone happened to Job."

He looked down and shook his head. "And Job didn't understand why it was happening to him." He walked across the stage, pointing at the audience. "Bad things can happen to you also. Kinda like what you thought may have happened to Herby. Some days you too may be in trouble. Something bad may happen to you, although probably not as bad as what happened to Job. You may be worried about something. It may be a bully at school. Or problems at home."

Bobby could relate to that. His older brother, Tommy, kept pushing him around at home. *But what can I do about it? Can't tell Dad. That'll just make Tommy mad. And I'll pay for that.*

"So here's your lesson for tonight," Mr. Seward said. "When you're in trouble, when you're scared of something, remember what Job's friend told him."

THE MAGIC OF GRACE

He turned in his Bible to Job 5:8–9. "If I were you, I would appeal to God; I would lay my cause before Him. He performs wonders that cannot be fathomed, miracles that cannot be counted."

He paused and closed the book. "If you tell God about it and ask Him for help, God will fix whatever's bothering you. He'll take care of it. Now He may not fix it like you expect, but He *will* fix it. All you have to do is trust Him. Do you all understand that?"

Bobby nodded.

"OK. Good. So whenever you see a rabbit, remember Herby and Job—and trust God no matter what. OK?"

"OK," they shouted in unison.

"I'll see you later, guys." He waved good-bye and left the stage.

The pack leader approached the microphone. He clapped his hands. "Let's have a big hand for Mr. Seward, boys." And to the magician he said, "Thank you, Drew. Excellent show."

The boys cheered.

Bobby slapped Danny on the back. "Your dad's really cool. Do you think he'll let me play with Herby?"

Danny smiled. "Sure." He smirked again.

"What's so funny? What's wrong with you tonight?"

"Nothin'." Danny was still smiling.

Off stage and out of the limelight, Mr. Seward, the part-time conjuror, reverted back to being just another typical dad on a Scout outing. He joined the other adult chaperones who watched from the side.

The scoutmaster came over to him. "Drew, that was a good lesson you taught tonight."

"Thanks. I was going to talk about Job to my Sunday school class this week anyway. I might even do the rabbit thing again."

Off to the side Drew noticed his friend Jim, who had carried Herby off stage. "And speaking of rabbit…excuse me for a moment." Drew gestured to Jim and moved away from the other fathers.

Jim discreetly handed Drew a paper bag. "You can have your rabbit back now, Drew," he whispered.

Drew chuckled with his trusted confidant. "Thanks. You know, my son, Danny, wishes we had a live rabbit for occasions such as this. But Mom put her foot down and refused. She didn't like the idea of rabbit droppings anywhere near the house."

He took "Herby" out of the bag. "So I ordered this from a magic catalog. See, I just press this button at the back of its neck, and presto." Herby wiggled and looked ready to hop away.

"That's something," Jim said. "Sure looks real to me."

Drew placed the rabbit back in the bag.

Later, another father approached Drew and patted him on the back.

"Good job, Drew," he said. "But I'd sure like to know how you made that card reappear in the frame"—he referred to a trick earlier in the show—"especially after you burned it up."

Drew smiled but didn't say anything.

"You didn't really burn it up, did you?"

"Now, John," Drew said, waving his finger as a parent would toward a naughty child. "You know I can't tell you how it works. That would violate the magician's code of conduct."

"I know, but—"

"Besides," Drew continued, "it ruins the effect. I realize you want to know now how it's done. But once you do, chances are you'll wish you didn't. Takes all the fun out of it."

"OK. I'll take your word for it."

Drew could tell he was disappointed and couldn't help but feel some empathy for him. He and John went back many years.

"Well…since you're such a good friend, I'll give you a couple of hints. You see, mirrors, when they're placed correctly inside a box, make objects look like they vanish and reappear. Likewise, something you may think was on fire may actually be tucked away somewhere safe, only to be shown again later."

"I get it," John said. "Smoke and mirrors."

"That's correct." Drew nodded.

Smoke and mirrors. That's all an illusion.

As he gazed into the bonfire, Drew recalled a particular summer many years ago when he'd given his first performance in a setting similar in many ways to the one here tonight.

A wise old scoutmaster had taught him the art of illusion. He thanked God that, in this case, the old man had violated the magician's code of conduct. And if he was somehow able to watch this scene tonight from heaven, Drew was certain he would be proud of him.

Not so much for the performance but for something more important.

He gazed up at the stars.

Did I do OK, Mr. Michaels? Have I used what you taught me like you wanted me to? To tell the true story about a God who is not magic but very much alive? I hope so.

And thank You, God, for bringing that old man and me together.

CHAPTER 1

THE BOOKSTORE AND THE MAGICIAN
Prevenient Grace

Drew Seward was from a small city nestled in the Shenandoah Mountains of western Virginia. He grew up in the early '60s, long before K-Mart and the city's first indoor mall came along. Back then, people went "downtown" to do their serious shopping. A popular song on the radio actually called downtown the place where "everything's waiting for you."

Along Main Street, folks could find just about anything they needed or desired: clothing stores, the main bank, Ben's Drug Store, Woolworth's, the barber shop, the beauty parlor, the pool hall, and other various and sundry stores. The town's only movie theater was on Main Street, where on Saturday mornings kids could get in to the matinee free with two cardboard milk bottle caps.

On one particular Saturday morning in the fall, Drew found he had nothing to do. His friend next door was away visiting his grandparents, and no one else in the block seemed to be around. Drew had some cash on him for raking leaves for the old woman down the street after school last week, and he wanted to spend some of it.

He went to his mother, who was washing the breakfast dishes. "Mom, is it OK if I go downtown for a while?"

"Is your room picked up?"

"Yes, ma'am."

"All right. Just be careful. And be home by noon. Your father and I are going out this afternoon."

From where Drew lived, Main Street was a little more than

two miles away as the crow flies. He often walked downtown rather than take the city bus. Walking was free. He strolled through his neighborhood and admired the color of the trees in the yards and along the sidewalks. Thanks to an unusually wet summer, the shades of brown and crimson were brilliant. He breathed in the fresh smell of autumn. The temperature was just right. Someone nearby was burning leaves, and the bittersweet fragrance blended perfectly with the crisp fall air.

What a perfect day, he thought.

When Drew was halfway there, the landscape turned more commercial with office buildings, factories, and stoplights. He strolled past the Dairy Queen.

An ice cream cone dipped in chocolate would taste pretty good right now. But I'd better save the money for later. I may need it.

He cut across a public parking lot, weaving through the cars and parking meters. A little farther, and Drew crossed the railroad tracks next to the bus station and finally turned onto Main Street.

Drew didn't stop to window-shop or browse. He knew exactly what he wanted and where to find it. What he came for would be found in a run-down, hole-in-the-wall place wedged between the movie theater and pool hall. The marquee over the Majestic Theater showed that *Shenandoah*, starring Jimmy Stewart, was currently playing. Considering the name and setting of the movie, it was sure to attract many of the area residents.

Two older teenagers came out of the pool hall next door and turned his direction. They wore blue jeans and white socks. One had a cigarette pack rolled up in the sleeve of his dingy-white tee shirt. Their hair was shiny and greased back.

Drew and his friends called guys like them rednecks but never to their faces. That could get a kid a fist in the face and maybe a missing tooth. As they drew closer, Drew nervously avoided eye contact and walked a little faster. But they paid no attention to him.

I hope I never run into them again, he thought. But something in his gut told him another encounter was guaranteed.

The door to the bookstore was propped open. He ducked in, relieved to be off the sidewalk in case they changed their minds and turned around to get him.

The inside of the store was dim and musty. The door had been deliberately left open to let in the outside air, although the extra ventilation didn't seem to make much of a difference. A ray of sunlight pierced a window, illuminating drifting cigar and cigarette smoke. Drew coughed as his lungs adjusted to the dramatic change in air quality.

Tall bookshelves lined the walls, filled with hardcover and paperback books. The owner and ex-librarian, Mr. Beauregard "Bo" Stevens, did a decent job of keeping them organized by genre and arranged in alphabetical order by the authors' last names. Two large, dark oak tables for reading sat in the center of the room. The rest of the furniture was a hodgepodge of mismatched chairs and floor lamps from thrift shops and junkyards.

At the back of the store, set apart from the library section, was a counter and three bar stools along with three small tables and chairs. As well as keeping track of books, Bo ran a minidiner, serving sandwiches, chips, and homemade desserts. Fresh-brewed coffee and soft drinks were available anytime during the day.

The bookstore had become a favorite gathering place for a few of the older locals who had known Bo for many years. They didn't care much for the books, but frequented the place to catch up on the latest news and gossip while enjoying a cup of coffee and a slice of apple pie. Some came to simply leave the world behind for a while.

As his eyes adjusted to the room from the bright outdoors, Drew saw Bo was busy behind the counter. He certainly didn't look like a librarian; he wore a dingy apron, and a lit cigar hung from his mouth.

"Hey, Mr. Stevens," Drew said with a wave. He was a known regular.

Bo looked up from drying a glass. "Well, young master Drew. What brings you here on this bee-oo-tee-ful morning? A cup of coffee and the newspaper, perhaps?"

Drew didn't come to chitchat. "C'mon, Mr. Stevens. You know I'm not allowed to drink coffee. It'll stunt my growth," he said, echoing his parents' warnings about coffee and cigarettes. "Besides, you know why I'm here."

"Ah, yes," Bo said. "Your beloved cartoon books. You know where they are."

Drew headed straight to an obscure, small bookshelf tucked away in a back corner. The shelf contained several stacks of used comic books. Each cost a nickel except the annual issues, which were a collection of the best stories of the prior year. Those were twenty-five cents.

Drew often bragged to Mr. Stevens about his huge collection of comic books. Batman was his favorite, followed closely by Superman, Green Lantern, and Spider-Man. He could easily spend the entire day searching through the stacks, looking to add to his large assortment at home. His greatest hope was to come across one of the rare first issues of *Detective* or *Superman*. Those were worth a lot of money.

He plopped down on the floor and took in the piles of comics waiting to be picked through. He took off his jacket and went to work, thumbing through the various covers of *Batman*, *Justice League*, *Green Lantern*, and *The Fantastic Four*. He came across a 1961 issue of *Batman* that featured the caped crusader's worst nemesis, the Joker. Drew looked over the first few pages to make sure he didn't already have this one at home. It didn't look familiar, so he set it aside to buy later and went back to his search.

Bo and another customer were arguing about who was responsible for the local high school football team's loss last night, the coach or the officials. Someone had turned on the large ceiling fan to clear the air; the motor hummed as the blades swooshed through the smoke. But Drew was oblivious to anything or anyone else in the store. He probably wouldn't have noticed if a masked robber suddenly burst in with guns blazing. Unless Batman showed up, of course.

Drew was so engrossed in the latest escapades of the Riddler that he didn't initially notice the pair of dirty, scuffed, brown wing tip shoes by his knees.

A voice above him said, "Hello, young man." The voice was raspy and hoarse, the distinctive sound of a heavy smoker.

Drew jerked up. An internal alarm went off in his brain that reminded him of his parents' constant warnings not to talk to strangers.

He stood up but kept his eyes on the floor. As with the rednecks, he didn't want to attract further attention by making eye contact with the stranger. Plus, he focused on figuring out the fastest way to the front door—just in case the situation turned bad, as his parents said could happen, and he needed to escape. Of course, if he ran, he'd need to abandon the Batman comic book he wanted. Hopefully, it would still be here tomorrow.

But once he was up, he couldn't help but look at the man's face.

The stranger was smiling. And though he looked a bit rough and disheveled, he seemed friendly enough.

Mom would say he's got kind eyes, Drew thought. Sort of like their beagle's eyes. Drew relaxed a little and reminded himself he wasn't alone. Mr. Stevens was still at the counter and could see everything going on. No need to worry.

The man wore a dark-brown overcoat. It was stained and spotted with burn marks, most likely caused by stray cigarette embers. A matching brown fedora tilted back on his head.

He held out his right hand. It was the same color as his coat with almost the same texture. His leathery palm had enough deep lines to keep a fortune-teller busy for hours.

"You ever seen this before, son?" the man asked.

He pointed at some coins he was holding. Drew counted one, two, three, four...four nickels. For a second Drew thought the man planned to give him twenty cents. That would buy four more comic books or two annuals, and that would be a good thing.

But he remembered his mother's warning.

Don't take money from strangers.

Or was it candy? Had to be candy, he decided, because money couldn't be poisonous.

With his left hand, the old man arranged the coins in a neat stack. He reached into his pocket and pulled out a small brass cover. He slid the cover over the nickels. Drew noticed his hand was a little shaky.

The man waved a hand over the cover and then—presto!—he removed it. The nickels were gone, and in their place lay a stack of dimes. He spread them apart.

Yep, four dimes. Instead of nickels.

Drew's jaw dropped.

How did he do that?

He had watched every move the old man made. The man even handed Drew the brass cover and told him to examine it.

He did and discovered nothing unusual.

So the only one way to find out "how" was…

Ask. So he did.

"Gee, mister. How'd ya do that?"

The old man chuckled. He didn't answer. Not a word.

Apparently, no secrets would be revealed today, no mysteries solved.

He put the coins back in his pocket and gently patted his awestruck spectator's head.

"Someday you'll find out. When the time is right."

Still smiling, he turned away.

"See you later, son," he said. Like a bird taking off, his brown coat fanned out behind him as he rushed out the door and vanished into the street.

During our lifetimes, we experience many things we do not expect. Occasionally they take us completely by surprise and catch us off guard. They happen "out of the blue." Like an ordinary autumn day, when a rumpled old man showed up in a bookstore.

He could have been a drifter or someone homeless and down on his luck. He just so happened to be on that street at that specific time and place when he decided to step inside. He saw a boy whose only interest that day was a five-cent comic book. But instead of spending an entire afternoon immersed in the world of superheroes, the boy met a man and witnessed a phenomenon he couldn't explain. Nor could he forget.

What if, on that same day, on the other side of town, someone from another city was visiting on business? The man was late for a meeting at an office building near where a kid named Donny lived. Donny was thirteen years old and, unlike Drew, allowed to ride his bike in the street. The businessman didn't see the stoplight when he sped his rental car into the intersection at the same time Donny was crossing it.

Two people with nothing in common—location or circumstances—happened to be at the same place at the same time. The outcome of their chance (?) encounter affected them both for years to come.

These out-of-the-blue encounters can have significant life-changing ramifications. Lives can be completely changed. Who would have ever thought that the goofy-looking guy who accidently bumped into Carol at the library, scattering her books and papers across the floor, would later become her husband and the father of their two beautiful children? Two lives would have never existed had not two people just "happened" to be at the same place at the same time.

How is it that these seemingly coincidental events happen? Why do they occur? Some people would say it's because certain stars and planets are lined up a certain way. But most simply don't know. They can't explain why. Things just happen.

"What a coincidence" is usually the best explanation they can come up with.

But was it? Was it just a coincidence?

Consider for a moment that maybe something more is causing those things that "just happen" in your life. Perhaps somebody or something is working behind the scenes. What you may attribute to luck or some other type of chance may actually be the result of a carefully conceived plan.

The One who created the universe has plans. God says He has a plan just for you. And His plan is for good and not for evil, to give you a future and a hope (Jeremiah 29:11).

God made His plan for you long before you took your first breath.

God saw you before you were even born.

Your DNA makeup didn't happen by chance. He had a hand in putting you together. God created you the way He planned you to be.

He also knows before you do what will happen on each day of your life. He knows your thoughts; He's with you when you wake up and when you go to sleep.

You see, God has a personal interest in you.

Starting with the first man He created, God intended for us to be His children, to be like Him, to be holy, loving, patient, wise, and faithful. To share a close and personal relationship with Him.

To be pure.

But as we all know, we didn't turn out that way.

He provided Adam and Eve a perfect environment, a paradise, where they enjoyed a one-on-one relationship with Him. He loved them and cared so much about them that He gave them the freedom to do almost anything they wanted. He took a risk by letting them make choices.

As we all know, they chose badly. They broke the one rule God had given them. Their action severed the intimate relationship they enjoyed with God. And that separation has carried on from generation to generation.

We were born destined to live in sin and apart from God. As Paul wrote in his letter to the Romans, "For all have sinned and fall short of the glory of God" (Romans 3:23).

But God still has a vested interest in each of us. Remember...

He created you. You have been wired with Him from the very beginning.

He wants to restore His relationship with you. You may not realize this, but God has been pursuing you. He will cause things to happen in your life that will lead you to Him. God's divine intervention in this regard is known as prevenient grace.

A good illustration of God's prevenient grace can be found in the book of Acts, chapter 10. During the time of the early church after Jesus Christ's resurrection and His return to heaven, a Roman centurion named Cornelius lived in Caesarea. This cosmopolitan city was the Roman capital of Judea and home to many important government officials. Cornelius was the high-ranking commander of the Italian regiment.

Cornelius was not Jewish, but he believed in God. He also knew nothing about Jesus. One day he had a dream or a vision. In his dream a messenger from God told him to send a group of men to the port city of Joppa to find and bring back a man called Peter. The messenger also told Cornelius exactly where to find Peter, who was living in a house by the sea.

This was the same Peter who was one of Jesus's disciples.

Cornelius did what God told him. He sent his servants to get Peter.

Shortly before Cornelius's men reached Joppa, Peter was hungry and praying when he fell into a trance. He saw animals, including reptiles and birds, being lowered from the sky on a sheet held by its four corners. A voice told Peter to kill the animals and cook them for a meal. Jewish law, however, forbade the consumption of these particular animals. So Peter refused the voice because the animals were impure and unclean. But the voice responded, "Don't call anything impure that God has made clean."

This vision occurred two more times.

After Peter awoke, the men arrived at the house, asking for him. When Peter learned why they had come, he understood the vision. God accepts everyone, regardless of their heritage or where they come from.

He returned with them to Caesarea, where he preached the good news of Jesus Christ to Cornelius and his entire family. Cornelius became a Christian.

God had prepared Peter to minister to Cornelius through a dream. If he had not had the dream, Peter probably would not have left Joppa with men sent by a Roman centurion. And by sending a messenger to Cornelius, God arranged for the Roman centurion to receive the truth about Jesus Christ through Peter.

To carry out His plan for you, as He did with Cornelius and Peter, God can and will create events that intersect your path. These are often unexpected or, as they say, "out of the blue."

So when something happens you never would have expected, such as a stranger suddenly showing up and changing nickels to dimes, the event may be more than just a coincidence.

CHAPTER 2

CAMP SEQUOYAH

Drew joined the Boy Scouts when he was eleven years old. The Presbyterian church sponsored Boy Scout Troop 35, and most of the boys in the troop, including Drew, attended the church.

John Williams, a church deacon, was the scoutmaster. Both of Williams's sons were Scouts and members of the troop. His eldest, Tommy, was an Eagle Scout, the highest achievement in scouting. Mr. Williams's youngest son, John, was Drew's age. During an award ceremony at the end of his second year in scouting, Drew watched Mr. Williams proudly pin the rank of Star on John as he stood in front of the troop. He had since earned two merit badges and was well on his way to making the next rank of Life.

Drew's father was also at the award ceremony. Afterward, on the way home, Drew worried he was going to miss his favorite TV show.

Couldn't you drive a little faster, Dad?

Dad asked, "When are you going to make Star, Drew?"

Here we go again. "I don't know, Dad. Soon, I guess."

"Soon? You'd better get with the program, Son. It took you almost two years to make First Class, which should have taken one."

"I'll do it at camp." *Now, please get off my case.*

Each summer, Boy Scout troops from Virginia, eastern Tennessee, and western North Carolina spent a week at Camp Sequoyah. Located near a national forest and other Virginia state parks, the camp was named after a famous Cherokee who had roamed the area in the 1700s. From June to Labor Day, Camp Sequoyah was home to hundreds of Scouts.

The camp had an abundance of natural and man-made resources, enough to keep a Boy Scout thoroughly occupied for the seven days and six nights there. The camp provided a natural environment where a Scout could earn many more merit badges than he could at home.

Drew's troop was scheduled to go in two weeks.

At the Tuesday evening Scout meeting prior to departing for camp on Sunday, Mr. Williams issued instructions to the anxious Scouts. Tommy stood next to his dad, clipboard in hand, checking off whatever needed to be checked.

During the two-hour meeting, the boys finished packing the troop's gear.

Drew was tired of the tedious cleaning, folding, and maintaining of the tents, lanterns, cooking equipment, hatchets, and countless other tools. He had spent his past two Saturdays at the church, working with the rest of the guys and getting ready to go.

Get this over with and let's get to camp. Mr. Williams takes the motto "Be Prepared" a little too seriously.

The meeting ended with Mr. Williams's brief and simple directive.

"Be at the camp's parking lot no later than fourteen hundred hours," he said. "I will meet you there." Fourteen hundred hours meant two o'clock in the afternoon and not a minute later.

Camp Sequoyah was only thirty miles away, but the difficult mountain roads made the drive more than an hour. The church owned an old school bus that normally took the Scouts to camp. Unfortunately, the bus's transmission had broken down during the church's last picnic outing. Jeff Aims, one of the more devout church members and a mechanic by trade, offered to rebuild the transmission for free. However, he had to do a special order on the part needed to complete the repair. It wouldn't arrive before the troop left for camp. The boys had to get there on their own, which meant most parents needed to forfeit their Sunday afternoon to drive them.

After the Scout meeting, Drew's mom was in the parking lot, waiting to pick him up. He jumped in the front seat of the family Buick and pulled out the handbook on Camp Sequoyah he carried in his back pocket. The handbook had been included in the packet of information and forms Mr. Williams had provided to each Scout weeks ago. Hardly a day had gone by that he hadn't looked through it at least once. The dog-eared pages were torn from wear.

Drew didn't care about anything else in the packet. His parents had filled out all the forms required for a kid to spend a week in the woods—details on vaccinations, known allergies, medications, hobbies, past illnesses like chicken pox, what the Scout couldn't eat, emergency contact names and numbers, and the list went on.

Drew was interested only in the book.

As his mom drove home, he switched on his penlight, a must-have at every Scout meeting.

Boy, I can't wait to get to camp.

For now, the pictures were the closest thing to being there.

He again flipped through the pages.

Oh, man. Miles of trails. And look at that mountain view. Canoes. Fishing. A guy with a bow and arrow. Campfires. Sleeping in tents. Lakes. This is so cool.

He looked out the window.

Only five days left, and I'll be gone for an entire week. And not a sissy, close-to-home, one-nighter. I'm going into the real boonies far from home. And the best thing—Mom and Dad won't be there.

His cousin, Jeff, who was two years older, worked as a counselor at Sequoyah.

Jeff sure is lucky. He gets to stay at camp all summer.

Drew planned to take advantage of his cousin's status.

I'll be able to hang around with him and all the cool, important guys.

Drew spent the next four days in anxious anticipation. He repacked and unpacked his footlocker a dozen times. He read the handbook about as many times until it no longer satisfied him.

Man, is Sunday ever gonna get here?

After what seemed like an eternity, the big day finally arrived.

Drew and his best friend, Jimmy, lived on the same block. Jimmy was a Boy Scout in a different troop. But since Jimmy's Troop 75 was going to Sequoyah the same week as Troop 35, Jimmy's mom volunteered to drive both boys.

Drew's mom decided to go along to keep her friend company; plus she could keep an eye on Drew without him getting all bothered, wondering why his mom had to come along. And Mr. Seward could enjoy the afternoon, working off his honey-do list or doing whatever he wanted on a Sunday afternoon all to himself.

After church, Drew and Jimmy went home and wolfed down cheese sandwiches and potato chips for lunch. They ran outside and quickly loaded their footlockers, bags, and backpacks into Jimmy's station wagon. Wasting no time, they were ready to leave much earlier than necessary and long before their moms were ready to go.

Rather than sit around bored like he had all week, Drew said to Jimmy, "Why don't you get your basketball? We can play some horse."

Jimmy's dad had built a goal and backboard on the garage above the driveway. The boys killed time and burned off excess energy shooting baskets in the driveway. But that lasted only for a short while. An adventure was waiting, and their patience grew thin. The calls for action went out.

"Mom! Hurry up," Drew called. "We're gonna be late!"

After what seemed like another eternity, their mothers appeared. The boys jumped into the backseat of the station wagon.

Unfortunately, the weather forecast appeared less than promising for the first day of camp. The sky was overcast, and the weather report in Sunday's newspaper predicted late afternoon storms.

Bummer, Drew thought. He hoped it would stay dry but kept that wish to himself. He knew better than to say anything out loud—that would jinx everything and guarantee a washout of tonight's big welcoming ceremony.

According to the handbook Drew had by now almost memorized, the first night's festivities would feature a huge bonfire. The older Scouts who worked at the camp dressed up like Indians and performed war dances, whooping and yelling to the beat of tom-toms. Drew could picture it in his mind and imagine their Indian chants. *Heyy yaah. Hey yah. Hey yah.* He would hate to see the ceremony canceled due to bad weather.

But after Jimmy's mom backed out of the driveway and they were on the road, eager anticipation kicked back in. Drew forgot all about rain.

Look out, camp! Here I come! Whoopee!

A few miles beyond the city limits, the mountain range that marked their final destination rose in the distance. Drew was unusually quiet during the trip, staring out the back windows at the passing scenery while their mothers talked about stuff he didn't understand or care about. He was dreaming about what lay ahead.

Jimmy asked his mother if she thought it was going to rain. "Boys, look at the sky," she said. "If there's enough blue up there to fill a Dutchman's britches, it won't rain."

Drew had no idea about how big a Dutchman's britches was, but a huge splotch of blue showed through the gray clouds. He and Jimmy giggled and thought up all sorts of funny things having to do with pants. Jimmy pointed at Drew and called him "fatty blue britches," to which Drew said, "Shut up, dweedledum," and hit him in the arm.

"You boys settle down," Drew's mother said. "You don't want

to get in trouble before camp starts. We don't want to have to take you back home."

She's just kidding, Drew thought. But to be safe, he scooted as far away from Jimmy as he could. Drew knew they were close when the car turned off the asphalt highway and onto a narrow gravel road. Wooden direction signs appeared on the side of the road, pointing the way to Camp Sequoyah. The trees closed in around them. A fresh smell permeated the air.

On Camp Sequoyah's one access road, the car dipped and swayed as Jimmy's mom cautiously maneuvered through the ruts. At one point, she had to pull off to the side to make way for an oncoming delivery truck leaving the camp.

After a couple of miles of stomach-turning maneuvers around huge bumps and deep holes, they finally broke out of the wood line and turned into a large gravel parking lot. Many cars and buses had already arrived.

"Good gosh," Jimmy's mom said. "How in the world did those big buses get through?"

As she maneuvered for a parking spot, Drew watched as parents milled about while their sons were busy unloading and carrying their gear to assigned areas. Scoutmasters scurried around, trying to gather their boys in one spot, a rally point marked by their troop's flag or guidon. They may as well have been herding wildcats.

Drew saw a not-so-enthusiastic Scout standing by himself, holding his troop's flag. His scoutmaster had probably drafted him for the job because he'd made the mistake of being the first one to arrive.

Drew jumped out of the car, eager to start exploring the rest of the camp, but his primary concern now was finding *his* troop's rally point. He didn't want to be counted as late. He soon spotted Troop 35's flag among many. After checking in with Mr. Williams, who seemed surprised and impressed to see him there on time, Drew rushed back to the car to get his gear and say good-bye to his mother.

She hugged him, kissed him on the cheek, and told him to behave. "Do everything Mr. Williams says. And be safe. We love you."

All Drew thought about was how cool this week was going to be. Freedom and fun stood out in his thoughts. Scouting was the last thing on his mind. Once he stowed away his gear in his tent, he planned to run off and find Jeff. See what his cousin was up to.

Drew hauled his stuff through the woods to Troop 35's campsite, his home for the next seven days. A damp smell in the air signaled a coming storm.

Bummer.

In a typical troop campsite, twenty or so tents were erected on wooden platforms. Each comfortably housed two Scouts with room for two cots, two footlockers, and enough space to move around. The scoutmaster had an even larger tent to himself, located away from the rest.

A smaller, wooden flagpole marked the center of the campsite, where the troop flew its own flag. Next to it was the burn pit, a large burned-out area surrounded by rocks. Here each evening, the Scouts started a bonfire, where their nighttime activities took place. The fire generated most of the illumination for the camp. Lanterns and individual flashlights made up the rest.

Drew located his assigned tent and carried his gear inside. Danny, his tent mate, had already arrived. "Hey, Danny! I made it. Ain't this great?"

Danny mumbled back. He was in the middle of blowing up the air mattress for his cot.

Drew dragged his footlocker into the tent. *This is just fantastic.* He could hardly wait for things to get started.

Then came the *pat-pat* sound of raindrops landing on the tent. A storm was approaching.

The evening bonfire and ceremony were cancelled.

SEVEN DAYS LATER

While the boys were at camp, the part for the bus transmission came in, and Jeff completed the job. On Saturday morning, the bus departed from the church to go pick up the Scouts.

In spite of a few nerve-wracking grinds and stalls, the bus made it to Sequoyah on schedule. Still, the driver prayed a silent prayer that it wouldn't break down somewhere on the way back in the middle of nowhere, carrying a busload full of anxious-to-get-home teenage boys.

By the time the bus arrived, the boys had finished loading all their gear in a large trailer. A father of one of the Scouts would haul it back behind his pickup.

The boys boarded the bus and Troop 35 headed home.

Drew and Danny sat next to each other, cutting up and laughing with the rest of the guys. Fifteen minutes into the trip, Mr. Williams stood at the front of the bus and made an announcement. And, of course, Tommy was there, too.

"Boys, I have a great idea. Here's what I want you to do." Mr. Williams explained. Starting at the front of the bus, each Scout was to stand and tell everyone his accomplishments during the past week.

"Tell us all what merit badges you earned," he said, "plus any special awards or achievements you received. And finally, what was the best thing you'll remember about your week at camp?"

Drew thought about what to say. His week at camp had been a blast. He'd gone to a lot of classes. He'd gotten to swim almost every day in the lake.

Canoeing was really great. And catching tadpoles. And playing softball.

Hanging around Jeff had been cool for a while, but soon his cousin started ignoring him.

I guess I shouldn't have bothered him as much.

"What are you going to say, Danny?" he asked his buddy.

Turns out Danny had earned enough merit badges to be promoted to Star.

The boy in the seat closest to the driver went first. He stood and turned to face the rest. He had to practically yell so the others could hear him over the vibration and whining of the gears as the bus crawled its way down the mountain.

"I earned five merit badges," he said. "Archery, camping, nature, cooking, and"—long pause—"oh, yeah, I almost forgot. Forestry."

The boys cheered.

"And the camp picked me to be on the color guard. I got to raise the flag one morning at reveille. I got the most advanced in swimming award and"—he held up a piece of paper—"here's my certificate to prove it. But I'm really happy I got picked to be in the Order of the Arrow."

The boys clapped and cheered again.

Drew wished he could disappear into the seat cushion.

One after another, the Scouts stood and spoke about all they had done during their week at Camp Sequoyah. Eddie, the troop's very own overachiever, annoyed Drew the most. Close to becoming an Eagle Scout, he was the same age as Drew. And he talked the longest, droning on and on.

This is gibberish. Drew wished Eddie would just shut up and sit down.

After Eddie finished his self-gratifying monologue, two more Scouts were yet to go, and then it would be Drew's turn. He hoped they would be back at the church before then, but that didn't seem likely.

I'm doomed.

Drew realized he had little to show compared to everyone else.

I earned two merit badges: first aid and canoeing. But everyone knows first aid is the easiest to get. And canoeing was not only easy but also fun. And everyone knows that, too. Especially Mr. Williams.

He supposed he could mention his relay team's first place in the swim meet, but dog-paddling twenty-five meters and balancing an egg on a spoon in his mouth didn't count for much. Especially compared to what the other guys had done.

The bus trip had just taken a turn for the worst in a close and personal way.

He would soon be embarrassed in front of his friends and Mr. Williams.

Then it dawned on him.

When I get home, Dad's gonna want to know what I did. And I promised him I would make Star. I didn't come close, and Dad's not gonna be happy.

The Scout seated in front of him went through his list of achievements and sat down.

Danny gently elbowed his buddy. "Hey, Drew. It's your turn, man."

Drew thought he might throw up his breakfast. He slowly stood up, swallowing back the nausea. He looked at the boys and Mr. Williams, who gazed at him expectantly.

Curious to hear what great things I did? Now what do I say?

He mumbled about how he had learned to stop bleeding and how he had uprighted an overturned canoe and won a relay race.

That's about it. Over and done. I need to sit down.

He stared at the floorboard to avoid seeing Mr. Williams's reaction. He didn't hear any clapping or cheers, although he did perceive what sounded like a snicker or two. He felt the bus seat shift when Danny stood up, but he didn't hear what he said. He wasn't listening.

What am I gonna tell Dad?

Drew's father was waiting at the church when the bus arrived. As the boys claimed their gear from the trailer, Drew glanced at his dad, who was talking to Mr. Williams. His dad was frowning.

They must be talking about me. I just know it.

His stomach knotted. He didn't want to get in the car and go home. He didn't want to think about what was going to happen when he got there.

Chapter 3

A SECOND CHANCE
Abundant Grace

Drew sat quietly in the front seat as his father drove home. Other than a terse "Welcome back" from Dad, neither had said a word since they left the church. Drew stared out the window, wishing he were somewhere else. The uncertainty of not knowing what was going to happen next made his stomach feel sick.

The old man's silence was a good sign he was going to blow a gasket. It wouldn't be the first time Dad's long silent spells came right before a storm erupted.

What did Mr. Wilson actually tell him? How did he respond? What did he say?

Drew could imagine how the conversation went. He had heard similar discussions many times before.

"He has the potential" and "If only he'd put some effort into (fill in the blank—homework, chores, sports, and on and on)" were the usual phrases. His dad would have said, "I don't understand why" because his dad said that a lot.

Mr. Williams would have said something like, "It's too bad because he's a really good kid," as several of his school teachers had done at PTA meetings.

He expected that the embarrassment he'd felt on the bus would be a piece of cake compared to what he would face when he got home.

He didn't have long to wait. His ordeal started as soon as the front door to the house closed. Dad went into rapid-fire mode.

"Do you mean to tell me…?"

"We spent all that money…?"

"You have nothing to show…?"

"You're no farther along than…?"

Rat-a-tat-tat. He barely paused to take a breath.

Drew took the verbal blows and said nothing. For a fleeting moment, he considered defending himself but wisely kept quiet. To say anything now would only make matters worse. Earning two merit badges hadn't impressed anyone on the bus, and it certainly wouldn't mean squat here. Especially with Dad's mood being what it was right now.

Mr. Seward took a short break to collect his thoughts.

"You know, Drew…your grandfather was an Eagle Scout. So is your uncle. What's the matter with you?"

Drew was well aware that his dad, too, was an Eagle Scout.

He continued. "Well, I hope you're proud of yourself." Then from out of nowhere came a vocal right cross. "At this rate, you won't make Eagle until you graduate from college." A stinging uppercut came next. "Who am I kidding? You wanna know something, Drew? I don't believe you'll ever make it."

This is not good, Drew thought.

He knew the difference between his father's anger and disappointment. He had been on the receiving side of both many times. But this was different. He discerned from Dad's tone that he was…sad. He suddenly realized he had not only disappointed his father but also let him down. This was a new thing for Drew. He actually felt pretty rotten about that. And for the first time in his young life, he was angry with himself.

He nervously waited for Dad's judgment, the real punishment, the actual price he would pay for his laziness and apathy. Would it be extra chores or a sacrifice of freedom—his allowance or the phone? Probably a combination of all of them.

Instead, Mr. Seward simply shook his head as if to give up, as if to say that everything he and his wife had said or done had had no effect whatsoever on their son.

"Well, you can't change what's already done," he said. "Get on up to your room and unpack. Don't forget to hang your sleeping bag in the backyard to air out. And you should take a shower.

Dinner will be ready in a few."

Drew walked up the stairs, head down and duffel bag still slung over his shoulder.

"Son."

Drew stopped and looked back over the banister.

Here it comes. He's gonna hand down my sentence. Now I'll know how I'll spend next week. Or maybe even next month.

"Yes, sir?"

"You could have done better. You do know that, don't you?"

No yelling. No screaming. Just his father calmly stating the truth. Drew nodded in sad agreement and went up to his room.

He dumped the dirty contents of his duffel bag onto the bed.

Dad had struck a chord. Drew knew he could handle lectures and groundings, but this was different. He wasn't sure how, but he knew he couldn't live with letting his dad down like this.

He flopped onto the bed, still feeling sick to his stomach. He rolled over and buried his head in his dirty camp clothes.

He knew of only one way to make things right. He needed to go back to Sequoyah.

All I need is one more chance, one more week. But how? I don't have the money to pay for it. I guess I could give up part of my allowance for a year. I can pay it back with the money from odd jobs around the neighborhood. I can get a paper route.

He sat up.

But how would I get there? Who would I go with? They won't let me go by myself.

He thought about how he would plead his case.

I promise to work harder. I'll make Life. I'll earn a fistful of merit badges.

OK, so Life might be a little too ambitious. (Life was the next rank above Star and would be practically impossible to accomplish in one week.) *But Dad would see I meant it this time, so that may sway him to OK a return trip.*

You won't be disappointed, Dad. You'll see I learned my lesson.

Please.

Will Dad believe I'm serious? I know Mom would, but I'm not too sure about him.

But the longer he thought about it...*Forget it,* he finally told himself. It was no use. Last week he'd had his one-and-only chance, and he'd blown it.

The best he could hope for was that this entire thing would soon blow over and that his father would forget it ever happened. But he knew that wasn't gonna happen.

But then again, it can't hurt to ask. All Dad could do is say no. And I might get some points just because I asked.

⊃⊂

While Drew contemplated how to approach his family to ask for a return trip to camp, his father sat in his basement office, wondering whether he should send his son back to camp. Would his son take the opportunity to better himself? He didn't hold out too much hope for that, but he was curious to see if his son would accept the offer.

A Seward Construction house had sold recently. With the extra income, his wife planned to buy a new freezer, one of those big stand-alone units so they could buy meats and other perishables by bulk. Counting that, some new clothes, and additions to their savings account, they could afford to send Drew back to camp for another week.

If he wanted to go.

⊃⊂

During supper, Drew played with his food and waited for the right time to bring up his idea of returning to camp. Mom and Dad talked about some new appliance they were buying next week.

Then Dad suddenly changed the subject. He stared directly at Drew. "How would you like to go back to camp for another week?"

Drew almost choked on the piece of meatloaf. Not sure what

he'd just heard, he looked over at Mom for clarification. She simply smiled.

"If you do," Mr. Seward said, "I'll look into finding a troop you can go with."

With his mouth full, Drew managed to mumble, "Uh-huh."

"But this time you'll have to do better. I expect some merit badges."

Drew nodded vigorously. He swallowed, and the words he had rehearsed earlier spilled out. "Don't worry, Dad. I'll do better. I promise."

"That's just talk, Son. What counts is what you do."

⋈

The next day, Mr. Seward checked with a close friend, whose church was sending a Scout troop to Sequoyah the coming week. Drew was welcome to go with Troop 103.

After Dad told him the news, Drew began to prepare immediately. He didn't waste time with the camp handbook. Instead, he read through the *Boy Scout Handbook* and picked out the merit badges he would work on. Knowing the camp and the normal daily schedule, he sketched a plan for how he would accomplish his goals.

Drew was still amazed Dad was sending him back to camp. Things just didn't work out like that. When he'd first thought about asking, he figured it was nothing more than a pipe dream, a wish that wouldn't come true.

He shook his head.

Life sure is surprising. You never know what's coming.

After a week of frivolous activity while wasting his parents' money, his father had given him a second chance. Drew would be able to make right something he had done wrong. Those opportunities do happen but not often.

⋈

What Drew experienced is known as grace. Grace is getting

something you don't deserve.

Jesus told a story about a young man who, like Drew, cared more about himself than about anything or anyone else. This boy demanded his father to immediately give him his inheritance; that portion of the father's estate would be his when his father died. As far as the son was concerned, his father was already dead. Although his request showed disrespect and selfishness, the father granted it.

The boy took the fortune and set out on his own to another country.

For a while, he lived a happy and carefree life, spending his money on wine, women, and song. Nothing was too expensive for him. He was having a great time, until one morning when he awoke and discovered he'd spent all his money. He was completely broke. To make matters worse, the land where he lived suffered a wicked drought. A severe famine raked the land. To survive, the boy had to find work as a common laborer. A pig farmer hired him to be his slave.

No union benefits came with this job. The meals he received were the same slop he fed the pigs. One day, as he rooted through a trough for anything edible, the boy realized he had hit rock bottom.

Then he came to his senses. He fondly remembered those days long ago at home, when even his father's servants were much better off than he was now. He longed to return, but was unsure whether his father would take him back after what he had done.

But he decided to go back home. According to Jesus, when he arrived, his father did welcome him back. In a big way. Seeing his son from a distance, he ran to greet him with more than just a handshake and a "Glad to see you, Son." The father threw a huge party in his son's honor and, on top of that, gave him expensive presents.

The father explained to the boy's older brother the reason for all the celebration. As far as he had known until today, his son was dead. But his son was thankfully alive. He had only been lost, but now they had found him. Who wouldn't be happy about that? (Luke 15:11–32).

The Greeks had a word for what the father did for his son. *Claris.*

Claris means a gift or kindness shown to someone who doesn't deserve it.

We know it as grace.

Drew's father was like the father of the Prodigal Son. Rather than punish Drew for his failures, he showed grace to his son. He gave him a chance to undo his wrong and turn it into right.

The Bible refers extensively to grace. In his letter to the Ephesians, the apostle Paul wrote, "For it is by grace you have been saved, through faith—and this is not from yourselves, it is the gift of God—not by works, so that no one can boast" (Ephesians 2:8–9).

God's greatest gift to us is His Son, Jesus. He sent Him to die for us, to take the punishment for the sins we commit. Jesus paid the price so God could pardon us and bring us back into a never-ending relationship with Him, the same relationship He intended to have with Adam and Eve.

All we need to do to receive this gift is believe it.

"For God so loved the world, that He gave His one and only son, that whoever believes in Him, shall not perish, but have eternal life" (John 3:16).

Chapter 4
THE SCOUTMASTER

The Scouts and parents of Troop 103 gathered at the church parking lot at 2:00 p.m. on Sunday. Unlike Drew's first trip to camp, this church's bus was in good working order, so the boys were going to camp together as a group.

Drew's father dropped him off. Before he left, he shook his young son's hand and challenged him. Not surprising coming from a former Eagle Scout, his words mirrored the Scout oath.

"Just do your best. If you do that, what you bring back as far as merit badges and rank doesn't really matter. Just as long as you give it an honest effort. You know what you're capable of and what you can do."

He ruffled Drew's hair. "See you in a week."

After his dad took off, Drew looked for whoever was in charge. He didn't see an adult in a Scout uniform; only a few parents waited while their sons horsed around.

He approached a group of Scouts to ask about a scoutmaster, but they were busy talking, and since he was a stranger, Drew didn't want to interrupt them. The boys were talking about their escapades and how much fun the summer had been so far. One Scout gave a somewhat- animated description of the girls in bikinis at the city's municipal swimming pool.

They also discussed how much fun the week ahead would be.

Drew wasn't interested in fun this time. He was on a mission. And the first thing he needed to do was find the scoutmaster.

But he couldn't find an adult in charge anywhere.

So here he was, on his own. Thrown in with a group of guys he didn't know. And he was as much a stranger to them as they were to him. He noticed several questioning stares as he walked around. He knew what they were thinking.

Who's that guy? What's he doing here?

Drew sighed.

How come there's no scoutmaster?

He wished Mr. Williams was here because he was quickly losing his once-eager anticipation and excitement for the upcoming week.

But things looked better when he saw Stevie Neese across the parking lot. Drew and Stevie's fathers had known each other for a long time. The families often got together for cookouts and other events.

"Hey, Stevie," he yelled. Happy to finally see someone he knew, he ran to greet his friend.

"Hey, Drew. My dad told me you were going to be here. They set it up so you and me could bunk together."

"That's great," Drew said. "This week's gonna be all right."

Finding a buddy in the midst of strangers improved Drew's outlook significantly, and he was again eager to get on with the adventure. Shortly after Drew and Stevie said hello, an older Scout announced for everyone to get on the bus.

"Let's move, people!" he said several times. He appeared to be in charge.

As Drew got in line to board the bus, the older Scout came up to him. "Are you the guy from the other troop?"

Drew nodded. "Yeah. I'm Drew Seward."

"OK. I was told to make sure you were here. Now get on the bus."

And that was Drew's welcome.

His heart sank. That wasn't much of a reception from the troop he would spend the next seven days with. He was obviously the new kid on the block.

Where was the scoutmaster? Drew wondered if Troop 103 even had one. The only adult on the bus was the driver.

After the troop arrived and checked into camp, roommate assignments were announced. Stevie and Drew moved their gear into their tent and prepared their cots. For the rest of the afternoon and through supper, the older Scout ran around, giving instructions.

Still no sign of a scoutmaster.

After the opening ceremony (the one that had been canceled during Drew's first week at camp), the boys retired to bed for the night.

As the sound of taps echoed through the woods, Drew lay wide awake in his sleeping bag. He had a hard time falling asleep. He worried and questioned whether he could actually accomplish what he had come here to do. He knew his concern stemmed from the fear of being a stranger in what seemed to be an unfriendly environment.

The next morning, Drew went with his new troop on an orientation hike to get familiar with the camp. The hike started early, right after breakfast.

The dew had yet to evaporate. The morning was bright, and the early morning air was fresh and crisp. The lush mountain foliage produced a pure and unique scent that couldn't be found anywhere else. Drew took it all in and felt the best he had since they arrived yesterday.

The single line of Scouts navigated the trails that crisscrossed the mountain terrain. The sun crept above the tree line, and single, orange rays of light pierced through the trees, accentuating the drops of dew clinging to the leaves.

At around the halfway point, the path went uphill for quite a long distance. Drew's thighs burned, and his breathing grew heavy as the hill grew steeper.

Drew trudged ahead. He shut out everything except the crunch of small twigs and brittle pine needles as he placed one foot in front of the other. He finally reached the top and crested the hill.

The downward slope now carried him along. His breathing returned to normal, and the dull pain in his legs subsided.

Drew was fired up, reenergized. For the moment, all was right with the world. He began planning his activities for the day. After this hike, he would get a break and clean up. Then he would go to his class on insects, where he would spend an hour combing the woods to find and photograph at least twenty different live species of bugs in their natural habitat.

After the last Scout reached the bottom of the hill, the troop stopped for a ten-minute break. Drew twisted out of the straps to his backpack and let it drop to the ground. He unsnapped the cover of an olive-drab carrier fastened to his web belt and pulled out his metal canteen. He plopped down by a tree next to Stevie and rested against the trunk. He unscrewed the cap and took a long drink. The water was still cold and refreshing.

From where he sat, Drew could see back up the hill he had just come down. Someone else, who had obviously fallen behind, appeared at the top and started to make his way down. He looked too old to be a Scout.

"That's our scoutmaster you've been asking about," Stevie said.

Drew watched as the man slowly made his way down the hill. For some reason, he stopped several times. But he finally reached the bottom and trudged past them. He wheezed and had difficulty catching his breath. He sucked in air, and his cheeks puffed out like a chipmunk's as he exhaled with a conspicuous *whoosh*.

Drew glanced away, not wanting to stare.

No wonder he's late and bringing up the rear. And haven't I seen him somewhere before?

Suddenly it dawned on him.

"Holy smokes, Stevie!" Drew said. "I've seen him before."

"How's that?"

"The bookstore. He's the man who changed the nickels into dimes."

"What in the world are you talking about?"

Drew gave the short version of the story, then asked, "Who is he? What's his name?"

"That's Mr. Michaels. Like I said, he's our scoutmaster."

CHAPTER 5

ON THE WAY BACK FROM BREAKFAST
You Are Not Alone

The troop posted today's and the next day's job assignments on a wooden bulletin board in the center of the campsite near the fire pit. After the orientation hike, Drew checked it. He saw his name listed for kitchen police, or KP as it was called in the army. He had been assigned KP for tomorrow's breakfast at the mess hall.

The campers ate three meals a day at the mess hall unless they were away from the main campground on a hike or overnight canoe trip. Each Scout was required to work KP for one or two meals in the kitchen during his week's stay. The job required him to report for his duty thirty minutes early. Later, after the rest of the campers arrived to eat, he would wait on three tables of thirty hungry and rowdy Scouts.

Good. I'll get KP over with early in the week and not worry about it anymore. Plus, it's during breakfast. If he had to miss a meal, he'd rather it be breakfast. Cereal and eggs were OK but not as good as sandwiches or meat and potatoes.

He read the rest of the announcements on the board and went to his tent to grab the supplies he needed for his bug class. On the way, he saw Mr. Michaels, who was slowly walking toward the larger scoutmaster's tent at the far side of the campsite. The scoutmaster was by himself. The other Scouts milled around the tents and didn't appear to notice or acknowledge him.

Strange. The man was supposedly in charge, but the Scouts acted like he wasn't even there.

For the rest of the day, Drew attended the required classes to reach his merit badge goals. Happy with his early progress, he promised himself he wouldn't let up.

As he headed back to the campsite to get ready for supper, the snap of a twig made him turn. Three guys were about twenty yards behind him on the same path.

Drew remembered them from lunch, sitting at the table next to his.

They were watching me awful close. And whispering about somethin'.

Drew had a knot in his stomach.

Wonder what they're up to.

He glanced over his shoulder. They were still there, eyeballing him and whispering.

What are they talking about?

Later that evening, when Drew and Stevie were turning in for the night, Drew got in his sleeping bag and told Stevie about his earlier encounter.

"Stevie, I saw these three guys on the bus when we came here. Tough guys. You know, like the ones who come from the projects on the south side."

"Yeah. They're rednecks. I see 'em after school. Smokin' and stuff. I stay clear of 'em."

"They were watching me at lunch today. And I think they were following me this afternoon."

Stevie sat up in his cot and looked over at Drew.

"You know somethin', Drew? In school one day, in the hallway, some poor kid got on their bad side. He didn't do nuthin' to 'em, maybe just looked at 'em the wrong way or somethin'. Anyway, they were waitin' for him after school. They ambushed the kid near the train station. Beat him up. For no good reason."

"Yeah, Stevie, I think I saw one of 'em before, too. Same day I met Mr. Michaels in the bookstore. He and some guys were near the movie theater."

"Well, just ignore 'em. They haven't bothered anyone in the troop. As far as I know, anyway."

Stevie turned off his flashlight. "You gotta leave early tomorrow morning, right?"

"Yeah. KP."

"Well, good night. And be quiet when you leave. Don't disturb my beauty sleep."

"Yeah, right. You sure ain't beautiful."

They both laughed. Camp was definitely fun.

Drew lay on his back and stared up into the dark.

Maybe they want to start a fight with me. But they wouldn't dare do that here, would they? We're at Scout camp. Things like that don't happen at a place like this. Scoutmasters wouldn't allow it.

Scoutmaster? What scoutmaster?

Ole man Michaels? As decrepit as he is?

He couldn't do nuthin' to stop them from beating me up.

The following morning, Drew woke before Stevie. The sun was barely peeking out from behind the mountains. He tried not to make any noise as he dressed quickly in the dim light. He slipped out of camp just as the rest of the troop was beginning to stir, taking the trail toward the creek. Behind him, the troop's bugler, still half asleep, missed several notes as he blew reveille.

A short hike later, Drew came to a small clearing in the woods where the dining hall had been built. Dingy gray smoke streamed from the metal chimney. He could almost taste the strong aroma of frying bacon. He hoped to grab something to eat before the rest of the camp arrived for breakfast.

He strode into the kitchen, where several fellow Scouts had arrived for duty and were wolfing down the first biscuits as quickly as they came out of the ovens.

Drew gathered with other servers, or "runners," around the head cook, who spat out instructions at lightning speed. His first lesson concerned the two wooden swinging doors separating the dining room from the kitchen.

"Always use the door to the right," the cook said.

The Scouts quickly learned that woe be it to the runner who used the left door to leave the kitchen at the same time another runner was coming, fast and furious, into the kitchen for refills. Each week, at least one Scout wore food instead of serving it.

Their first task was to set the tables with plates, glasses, silverware, and condiments such as ketchup, butter, syrup, salt, and pepper. By the time Drew was finished, he paused to brush the sweat off his forehead. Then he helped haul pitchers of fresh orange juice and cartons of milk from the refrigerators to the tables.

Just as Drew and his coworkers lined up behind the doors to the dining room, loaded with platters of steaming eggs, pancakes, and bacon, the mess hall doors opened. A herd of almost two hundred Scouts thundered inside. Chaos ensued as Scouts engaged in horseplay before scurrying to their assigned seats, unleashing the boyish energy stored up after a few hours of sleep. Roving counselors and scoutmasters herded them to their assigned tables.

Once they found their seats, the boys settled down as the camp chaplain approached the podium to give the blessing. Like he did every morning, he reminded the Scouts that *he* didn't bless the food.

"God does that," he said. "I just facilitate the process. Let us pray."

Drew braced himself. The head cook had told them that the chaplain's "amen" was like a starting gun going off at a track meet. No kidding.

"Bless this food to the nourishment of our bodies and us to Thy service. Amen."

Bang!

The doors between the kitchen and the dining room swung open, and they charged into the dining area with their trays of steaming food.

A runner couldn't carry enough trays of food fast enough to satisfy the ravenous campers. Drew was soon out of breath trying to keep up. He had to practically run back and forth between his assigned tables and the kitchen, replenishing trays, bowls, and pitchers as quickly as he could. Sweat stung his eyes, blinding him.

At one point, he paused and shook his arms to get the blood flowing again.

Good thing I ate something earlier. Gosh, how much longer do we have to go?

"Hey, runner! Bring more juice!" and "We want more pancakes!" rudely interrupted his break.

And instead of, "Thanks, pal," the usual response was, "What took you so long?"

Not only did Drew get grief from the campers; he got it from the cooks, too. The camp employed three full-time chefs, who ruthlessly ran the entire meal operation from start to finish. They drove the runners hard and offered little help and much less sympathy. Two of them constantly smoked cigars, which added a distinctly heavy tobacco aroma to the rest of the kitchen odors. Drew gagged a couple of times in the kitchen when he picked up a plate of soggy scrambled eggs.

While rushing through the kitchen to grab a pitcher, he accidentally bumped into one of the cooks.

"Hey, kid! Watch where you're friggin' goin', idiot!"

At one point between the kitchen and dining room, Drew asked his fellow runner, "What cave did those guys in the kitchen crawl out of?"

"Shhh! Not so loud," the Scout answered. "They were cooks in the army. Can't you tell from the tattoos?" Drew had noticed their large, hairy arms covered with what seemed to be army-type insignias.

"I don't blame 'em for being mean," the Scout said. "If I had to put up with two hundred screaming kids three times a day, I'd be grumpy, too."

"I guess you're right," Drew said.

Maybe I'll say somethin' nice to 'em later.

Whenever a short break in the action occurred, Drew followed his fellow runners into the kitchen and gobbled up whatever little scraps remained on the platters. They would have to wait until the next meal, the head cook said, to make up for the one they missed.

Drew looked forward to the next meal. Then the tables would be turned, so to speak. On the next-runner shift, he could holler at the Scouts, the ones who were hollering at him now.

The Golden Rule apparently didn't apply when it came to KP.

Although the major KP ordeal seemed to last much longer, it ended twenty minutes after the chaplain's "amen." Drew gratefully heard the ring of the bell that signaled breakfast was over. Time to go.

Almost. The head cook told the runners earlier they couldn't leave until he was satisfied that the dining hall was ready for the lunchtime shift.

As the Scouts filtered outside, Drew cleared his three tables and carried dirty dishes to the kitchen. He scraped the leftovers into large metal garbage cans and stacked the dishes for the dishwashers. He wiped down every table and neatly arranged the chairs.

His tables passed inspection. The head cook told him he could go.

Drew thanked the man before he left.

※

His KP duty finished, Drew excitedly headed for the exit doors. His cousin Jeff was waiting for him outside.

"Hey, Drew. What are you doing back here?"

"Hi, Jeff. I needed to earn some more merit badges, so Dad let me come back for another week."

"Great. What are you working on?"

"Well, this morning I have my first class in rappelling."

"Wow! Good for you. Mountain climbing isn't easy. How are you with handling ropes?"

"To tell you the truth, Jeff, I'm scared to death. I'm not looking forward to rappelling."

Climbing up a mountain or cliff was only half of the equation. To get back down required a Scout to rappel, or basically walk backwards, from the peak to the bottom, holding onto a rope.

Jeff waved his hand, brushing aside Drew's concern.

"Aw, don't worry. Rappelling is the easiest, and safest part."

Easy for you to say. I'm still afraid to climb up to the tree house Dad built in the backyard. And all that will keep me from crashing to the ground is a rope?

Just from thinking about that, Drew's stomach was churning. Again.

Jeff changed the subject. "What troop are you with now?"

"Troop 103 from Grace Methodist Church."

Jeff thought for a moment. "I've heard about 103. Be careful. There were some troublemakers in that troop who don't actually go to the church, and, if I remember right from last year, they caused some problems with some of the counselors. Don't know if they're still there or not."

"I'm pretty sure I know who you're talking about." Drew thought of the three campers who had been following him. "I'll stay clear of them for sure."

"Good idea," Jeff said. "And good luck. Come by if you need anything."

"Thanks."

Drew headed back to the campsite. He was almost halfway back to camp when the trail took a slight bend to the left next to a huge oak tree.

Ironically, one of the boys his cousin and he had just talked about suddenly popped out from behind the tree, blocking Drew's path. Drew was taken by surprise, but that feeling was quickly overcome by fear.

What's he doing here?

Then another boy appeared from the other side of the path. From the wicked sneer on his face, Drew knew this wasn't meant to be a friendly encounter. Unfortunately, his self-protective instinct to turn and flee came too late.

The first bully rushed Drew and pushed him in the chest. Drew's feet flew up above his head as he tumbled over backwards thanks to a third bully, who was down on all fours behind him.

The three guys had obviously planned this opportunity when Drew would be by himself. They'd executed their ambush with precision.

Drew hit the ground, his breath knocked out of him. They were on top of him. They pinned his arms and legs to the ground.

The guy who had pushed him looked down at him with a sneer. "Hey, dirtball. You think you know everything? What makes you think you're smart enough to be in my troop?"

Another chimed in. "Yeah, punk. Who do you think you are, anyway?"

"You ain't nuttin' but a sissy!" the third bully said.

Drew panicked. He gritted his teeth, struggling to free himself. It was no use. They held him down good. His arms started to numb. His eyes stung from the sweat off his brow. His only option was to lie still and wait for whatever they had in store for him. He hoped for mercy but braced for the first blow.

They grabbed his ankles, and suddenly his feet were off the ground above his head.

"You ain't been initiated yet," the apparent leader announced. They pulled off his shoes.

Drew realized what was coming. Or coming off.

"Let me go!" he yelled and kicked.

"Shut up!" One of the bullies clamped his palm over Drew's mouth.

"Hold him still."

"I got him, Rob!"

Drew felt helpless. They took off his Scout kerchief, then pulled off his shirt and pants. They dropped him back to the ground.

He sat on the damp grass in only his underwear and knee-high olive-green socks. He felt awful and humiliated.

Why don't they just leave me alone?

He fought back a tear.

I will not cry...I will not cry.

He looked up at his assailants. The one they called Rob was wadding up his clothes.

Drew didn't move. He sat quietly. They appeared to be finished, and he didn't want to risk standing up just to get knocked down again.

"If you want your clothes back, slime ball, I'll give you a little hint where you can find 'em," Rob said. "B. O. C."

Three letters.

"Got it?" he said.

Drew had no idea what that meant. But to avoid further confrontation, he nodded.

"B. O. C," he said.

And as quickly as they had appeared, they were gone. They ran off into the woods, along with his clothes.

Drew shook his head in relief.

They're gone. For now, anyway. It could have been worse. I still have my underwear and socks on.

He got to his feet and brushed off the leaves and dirt. Realizing he was wearing only his dew-moist skivvies, he scrambled off the path and slipped into the woods. He planned to sneak back to camp, hoping no one would see him in his current state. That would be hard to explain. Not to mention embarrassing.

He gingerly made his way back to the campsite, wishing now that he'd thrown all caution to the wind and used the path. His feet were raw and sore from walking without shoes across the carpet of dry pine needles, twigs, and rocks. With each painful step, the madder he became as he thought about what had happened.

"Why did they do this? I didn't do nothin' to them," he muttered. Suddenly it dawned on him—he still had almost a week of camp left.

Are they done messing with me? Taking my clothes was bad

enough, but are they planning something else? Will they attack again, or is my—what did they call it?— initiation…done?*

He thought of something else.

What does B. O. C. mean?

He snuck back into the campsite close to his tent. Thankful that no one had seen him, he slipped inside. Thank goodness, Stevie wasn't there.

Drew removed a fresh Scout shirt and a pair of shorts from his footlocker. Luckily, he had packed extra shoes, a pair of moccasins his folks had bought him for his first trip to camp.

He dressed quickly, realizing that if he didn't hurry he would be late for his rappelling class. But while he raced to get out the door, something told him to slow down for a minute. He stopped and sat down on his cot. A sense of calm swept over him.

"Bridge over the creek" jumped into his mind. From out of nowhere.

B. O. C. stands for "bridge over creek."

He had no idea what made him think of that.

Where did that come from?

He had to cross a creek on the way to the cliff, where the climbing class would be taught. It was the same creek he crossed every day to go to the mess hall.

He dashed out of the tent and took off at a dead run. When he reached the footbridge, he sidestepped it and slipped down the bank so he could look underneath. Jammed into the space where the bridge met the bank was a bundle of clothes.

His clothes. Along with his shoes.

He couldn't believe it. He'd sort of thought, and even hoped, his clothes were there. But he was still amazed they were actually where he'd thought they would be. And he didn't understand how he knew.

He gathered up his belongings.

How in the world did I figure that out?

It didn't make sense.

He didn't have enough time to take his stuff back to the tent, so he stashed the clothes in a nearby hollow stump, hidden away from the path. He would come back after dark to pick them up.

⊰⊱

After the Scouts finished their training for the day, the troop returned to the campsite to clean their gear and prepare for dinner. Drew was heading toward the latrine when Rob, the leader of the three-man gang that had ambushed him, approached him from the side and cut him off.

Drew tensed, ready to run if necessary. Or fight back if he had to.

But surely the guy wouldn't try anything here, not in the middle of camp, where there were plenty of witnesses. Besides, Rob was by himself now. The odds weren't as favorable as the three-to-one he'd had this morning.

Rob sneered. "Hey, kid. Did you find your stuff?"

Drew thought for a moment. Why was he asking that question? Maybe they'd gone back to the bridge and discovered that his clothes were gone.

He decided to give Rob and his buds something to think about.

"Nope." He shook his head. Then he threw in something else for them to worry about. "My dad'll be pretty mad when he finds out, too. He'll wanna know what happened."

He immediately wished he hadn't said that. Rob was probably thinking he'd squeal on them.

Now they'll kill me for sure.

Just as he feared, Rob raised a fist and shook it in his face. "You'd better keep your mouth shut if you know what's good for you."

"I won't tell anyone," Drew said. "I promise."

⊰⊱

During dinner and the evening campfire, Drew sensed the bullies were watching his every move.

Taps sounded after everyone had turned in for bed. For the second night, Drew had a hard time falling asleep. Every possible scenario raced through his mind.

What if they haven't gone to the bridge yet but go now and see the clothes are gone? If they figure out I lied to them, they'll think I lied about not tellin' on them. Are they going to beat me up tomorrow?

The "what if" tape played over and over in his head.

Gotta be careful. Can't let them catch me by myself.

I should tell the scoutmaster. But who? Old Mr. Michaels? What could he do? He was never around. Besides, he was too old and decrepit.

And I can't tell what's-his-name, the older Scout who spoke to him at the bus. *I sure don't trust him.*

Drew didn't know who else to talk to about his problem. Except his tent buddy, who was already asleep.

I'll break my promise and tell Stevie tomorrow morning. Maybe he'll know what to do.

He couldn't remember feeling as lonely as he did now.

※

But Drew was not alone.

All of us sometimes feel like we're on our own. We may see ourselves going it alone against any particular challenge we face. Maybe it's because no one is there to help, no one cares to help, or we're too embarrassed or proud to ask for help.

And though any of those reasons may be true, God will never leave us to fend for ourselves.

David was one of the most famous kings of ancient Israel. God picked him to be the future king when he was just a boy, and through His grace and providential intervention, He set the wheels in motion that would lead David to the throne.

Saul was the ruler of Israel at that time, and he contracted a disease, sent by God, that caused him stress and great anxiety.

David was well-known throughout the area as an accomplished harp player. An advisor to Saul knew of David's talent and suggested he summon the boy to his palace to play. Perhaps the soothing music would relieve the stress.

After David came and played for him, Saul was cured. So he hired David to be a permanent member of his staff (1 Samuel 16:14–23).

Israel was at war against the Philistines, and David's brothers were soldiers in the Israeli army. Shortly after David came to Saul's palace, David visited his brothers on the front line. While he was there, a giant Philistine soldier named Goliath came into the valley separating the armies. Days earlier, Goliath had challenged the Israelis to send their best and brightest soldier to fight him one-on-one. The winner would determine the outcome of the war—an all-or-nothing proposition. But no Israeli dared to volunteer.

David announced he would take care of the Philistine. As far as he was concerned, the giant was no more dangerous than the wolves or lions that went after his father's sheep. And David protected the sheep.

He went to a creek and picked up five smooth stones. Armed only with his staff, the stones, and a slingshot, he walked into the valley to face the giant by himself.

But David was not by himself. He knew God was with him.

David flung the only stone God would need from the sling, and He guided it through the air. It struck Goliath in the one spot on his forehead not protected by armor. The mighty Goliath went down. David finished him off, and the victory was Israel's (1 Samuel 17).

David's popularity among the Israelis grew so that King Saul worried that David had become a threat to him and his position as king. The king decided to take David out of the limelight permanently by killing him.

Fearing for his life, David fled into the wilderness. He spent months hiding out in caves as Saul and his men pursued him.

At first, David was by himself and scared. "Look and see, there is no one at my right hand; no one is concerned for me. I have no refuge; no one cares for my life" (Psalm 142:4).

But David realized God cared what happened to him when no one else did. He knew that God would see him through his ordeal. "Even though I walk through the darkest valley, I will fear no evil; for you are with me" (Psalm 23:4).

Like David, we can be assured that God is looking out for us, and He is more powerful than anything or anyone in this world that can come against us.

God is with you, and He is watching what happens to you. And He is always thinking about what's best for you.

He's in your house or in your tent. He's in your office or in the alley you are sleeping in tonight. He's riding in your car or sitting beside you in some lonely place.

Drew was never by himself. And neither are you.

Chapter 6
NIGHT ATTACK

The next morning after breakfast, Drew and Stevie were preparing for their first class when Drew told his tent mate about yesterday's encounter with the three bullies.

Stevie asked Drew how he was able to find his clothes. "How did you figure out what B. O. C. meant?"

"I don't know, Stevie. It just came to me. But I was scared, man. I'm afraid they are going to come get me again, since I found my stuff. And Stevie, you can't tell anyone I told you about this. If they find out, they'll kill me for sure."

Stevie stood up and pointed at Drew.

"Look, man. Don't worry. I won't say anything, and I'll be watching your back. If the jerks try anything, they'll have to deal with both of us."

"Thanks, man. You're a true buddy."

"OK, buddy. Let's move. We're gonna be late."

Drew was very cautious for the rest of the week. He remained on high alert and stayed as far away from the three bullies as possible, particularly during periods when he was most vulnerable, such as the troop's overnight canoe and camping trip. Walking to the mess hall and other camp areas was risky, too. He always tried to be with someone and never be alone.

And Stevie stayed true to his word. He became an ever-present shadow, always there and watching for trouble. No more attacks occurred during the rest of the week. On the last night of camp, Sequoyah conducted a camp-closing ceremony around a huge bonfire set up near the parade field. The primary purpose was to recognize those boys who had distinguished themselves during the week in some form or fashion. Many awards were presented that acknowledged individual excellence in various scouting and athletic activities, from hiking and swimming to track and field.

Drew laid out his Scout uniform on his cot. He checked it over carefully to make sure it was fit for inspection in case he was called forward for any recognition. But deep inside he didn't expect anything. Each troop nominated and selected their awardees, and Drew suspected his name wasn't on the list. He was still an outsider, but that was OK with him. He had nothing to prove to these guys or anyone else except himself, and he'd done that.

Later, Stevie sat on his cot, rubbing some leather cleaner over his moccasins.

"You know, Drew, you did pretty good this week, considering what happened with those knucklehead dweebs." Stevie chuckled over his reference to the three bullies.

"Yeah, Stevie, you got that right. Dweebs."

But I'm sure not gonna call them that to their face.

"So, what did you end up with, all told?" Stevie asked.

"I got five merit badges, and I just have a little more to do when I get back home to get three more."

Drew turned toward Stevie and held up his arms as if holding onto a rope.

"And hey, man, I even rappelled down a cliff! I couldn't believe it! I was scared to death, but it was easy."

"You should be qualified for Star rank, right?"

"Yeah, I should get that next week sometime, back with my own troop."

And Dad will be there to see it. And Mr. Williams is going to be proud of me, too. Cool.

Unlike the last time he was at Sequoyah, he had done much better than most of the troop. This past week his priorities were where they should have been all along. He had done what he set out to do, and he was pretty happy about that.

Mother Nature decided to storm on the last night of camp. The weather report called for nasty weather late in the day. Due to the threat of severe thunderstorms, the camp director decided to move the closing event to the large Scout hall.

Drew sat with the rest of the troop next to Stevie. He noticed Rob and his two buddies sitting in the row in front of them on the other side of the aisle. They were cutting up but didn't appear to be paying any notice to him or Stevie. That was good.

The ceremony lasted about an hour, interrupted occasionally by flashes of lightning and thunder booms. Drew was bored and didn't pay much attention to what was happening on stage. Rather, he thought about the past week and all that had happened.

Boy, I'm glad this is almost over. Tomorrow, I'm heading home. I'll be sleeping in my own bed again. Won't have to worry about the three goons anymore. I'll be back with my old troop and my real friends.

After awards were handed out, the camp director gave his closing remarks. "Boys, be safe as you prepare to leave tomorrow morning. And I hope to see each one of you again next year."

I bet he doesn't include those three "dweebs" sitting in front of us, Drew thought. He snickered. *Dweebs. I like that name.*

The chaplain came forward and gave the benediction, praying for the boys' protection as they went home and asking that God would be with them now and forevermore. Amen.

Under a steady downpour, Drew and the rest of the boys sloshed through the woods, heading for dry tents and sleeping bags. Scores of flashlight beams penetrated the night; rays of light lit up the rain as they sliced back and forth through the trees. The rat-a-tat sound of rain slapping against Drew's nylon poncho, combined with more than a hundred more sets of rain gear, sounded like a platoon of soldiers with machine guns.

Before going inside their tent, Drew and Stevie shed their rain gear and muddy galoshes to keep the inside as dry as possible. It was late, and Drew was tired; he didn't bother to fire up the lantern. And Stevie didn't care. He was already in his sleeping bag and asleep before Drew had stripped down to his underwear and crawled into his. Drew turned off his flashlight, and as soon as his head hit the pillow, the sound of the rain softly plinking against the tent lulled him to sleep.

A disturbance outside, close to the tent, interrupted the calm night. Drew stirred and opened one eye, not quite fully awake.

What's that?

Drew didn't have to wait long for the answer. The wooden floor shook when a gang of boys burst into the tent. His cot rattled. Drew raised his head.

What the heck is going on?

It was dark, but Drew had a pretty good idea who it was. And why they were here.

One of them turned on his flashlight and pointed it at Drew's face. The light blinded him; he couldn't see who it was.

But he sure recognized the voice.

"Will you look at this," Rob said. "The babies are already snug in their beds."

He's right. And we're trapped in our zipped-up cocoons. They're gonna kill us.

But being caught in their sleeping bags turned out to be a good thing for Drew and Stevie.

"Hey, Rob," one of the leader's cronies said. "It's not right to beat him up while he's in the sack all tied up."

Drew breathed a sigh of relief.

At least one of them has a sense of fairness. Maybe Rob will change his mind after he realizes that thrashing a kid who can't defend himself would be considered sissy by other bullies.

"Yeah, you're right," Rob said.

He placed the flashlight under his chin. His face glowed reddish-yellow. Drew thought for a second he was looking at the Devil.

Maybe I am.

Rob glared down at Drew.

"We'll be back soon, punk. And you both better be ready for us!"

And with that, they turned and left the same way they had come, disappearing into the dark, wet night.

All was quiet inside the tent, except for the *plink, plink* of the rain and heavy breathing.

Drew preferred to stay just where he was. The sleeping bag was warm. Maybe not safe, but comforting. He'd forgotten all about Stevie until a huge commotion came from his roommate's side of the tent.

Stevie unzipped and scrambled out of his sleeping bag, throwing it aside. He got up, ready for action.

"OK, that's enough!" he said. "They've crossed the line now! They wanna mess with me, too, huh? Let 'em try it. Come on, Drew. We're not going to take this lyin' down!"

And just because the bullies weren't in the tent anymore didn't stop Stevie from letting them know his intentions. He opened the tent flap and yelled into the night.

"Come on! We'll be ready for you."

Stevie fired up the lantern. He pulled on his pants and reached into the front pocket. He took out his trusty Scout pocket knife, a lock back with a three-and-a-quarter-inch blade. Drew watched his friend open up the blade. "Hey, man," he said. "Put the knife away. You could hurt 'em real bad."

"Don't worry," Stevie said with a laugh, flipping the knife in his hand. "Although I'd like to, I don't plan on cutting 'em."

He closed the knife and laid it aside. He reached into his backpack and pulled out a rock he had picked up during his geology merit badge class.

"Instead, I'll just throw this at the first one that dares to come in here," he said. "Maybe it'll bean his head and make him think twice about messin' with us."

Stevie became quite serious when he looked down at Drew,

who was still in his sleeping bag and feeling pathetically weak.

"You'd best get up and get ready," he said. "Your being in the sack ain't gonna stop 'em this time."

Drew reluctantly unzipped the bag and swung his feet to the floor. "OK, OK." He let out a nervous laugh and slowly pulled on his pants.

"Here's the plan," Stevie said. "We don't wait for them to attack. The second that flap opens, hit them with everything we got." Stevie gripped the rock, heavy enough to smart if it hit someone. "I'll throw this and then...What are *you* going to use?"

"I don't have anything," Drew said sheepishly.

"Well, find something! Gee whiz! Wait. I got an idea. Take off your belt."

Drew undid his belt and slipped it from his waist.

"You stand over there by the side of the door," Stevie said. "I'll get the first one through, and then you whack the next one with the belt. You understand?"

Drew nodded. "Yeah, I got it." A sudden burst of adrenaline fired him up. He slapped the belt against his thigh, his heart racing. His confidence level was way up there now with Stevie beside him.

"Let's do it," Drew shouted. We'll let 'em have it!"

"Shhh! We can't let 'em sneak up on us. Be quiet and listen." He whispered, "You watch the back. I'll watch the front."

All was quiet inside the tent. Drew stilled and stared intently at the rear opening to the tent.

POP!

Drew jerked.

What was that?

Another distinct popping sound came from outside...very close to the tent.

"Get ready," Stevie said in a low voice.

Drew tensed. He gripped the belt, prepared to defend himself. And waited.

Nothing.

POP!
He jerked again, drew back the belt.
The canvas tent was still.
All was quiet. The only noise was the gentle rustle of leaves as a light evening breeze blew through the camp.
Time passed. Nothing.
Drew's eyes grew heavy. The belt sagged by his side.
Suddenly a commotion came from the front of the tent.
Drew whirled around. Stevie pulled back his arm. He yelled, "Here they come!"
Before Drew could blink, the tent flap flew open.

※

God can show up when you least expect Him.

During his youth, Drew learned all about God. Sunday school and church attendance were mandatory for him and his little sister. His family was at church almost every Sunday morning and evening, along with Wednesday night Bible study.

His parents made sure he actively participated in church activities. He memorized the answers to all 107 questions in the *Westminster Shorter Catechism*. He sang in the youth choir. He knew the Apostles' Creed by heart. He knew the books of the Bible and their order. He was elected president of his senior Sunday school class.

For the most part, Drew was a pretty good kid. He behaved at school and rarely got into trouble. He respected older people and was very polite...a "yes, sir" and "no, ma'am" kind of guy. Adults who knew Drew through school and church liked him.

One year he and his parents attended an evening worship service during a week-long city revival, held in the local university gymnasium. At the end of a fire-and-brimstone sermon, the Baptist preacher called for all who wanted to be saved and accept Jesus Christ as their Savior to come forward.

The choir sang. Drew stood up, walked to the front, and joined the others who felt the same calling. His mother softly cried.

Drew went up primarily because he thought it was the right thing to do.

His summer at Camp Sequoyah became a distant memory. Drew graduated from high school. His choice of college and ensuing career took him away from his hometown for good. He left behind his parents, teachers, and his home church.

He still remembered God, but he had built his foundation on doing what others thought he should do. He strived to please others; he worried much about what they thought.

When one lives in a fallen world surrounded by temptations, that type of shallow foundation doesn't hold up very well or very long.

Shortly after graduating from college, he got married. He had a good job. He made a decent living. He and his wife had two children.

The Seward family went to church most Sundays...It was the right thing to do.

As the years went by, Drew became dissatisfied with most everything in his life. His marriage was boring. Raising two kids was OK, but it was more of a chore than a joy. His career wasn't meaningful or fun, but it did offer security in the form of a steady paycheck.

His unhappiness led to misery, and by then he totally ignored the God he had learned about during his youth. He became more self-centered and insecure.

Drew withdrew more into himself. He made bad choices, and turned to alcohol and other addictions to fill the void in his life

The bullies he'd encountered at Scout camp were nothing compared to the ones that now tormented him.

Paul wrote to the church in Galatia, "When you follow the desires of your sinful nature, the results are very clear; sexual immorality, impurity, lustful pleasures, idolatry, sorcery, hostility, quarreling, jealousy, outbursts of anger, selfish ambition, dissention, division, envy, drunkenness, wild parties and other sins like this" (Galatians 5:19–21 LB).

Drew followed his desires.

His decisions went from bad to very bad.

He now was totally separated from those things that at one time had been good things in his life—his family and friends. He had ripped apart relationships as if he had gone through them like a buzz saw.

But God was watching. He was there. All the time.

God has a patient but persistent manner. To move us close to Him, He uses events that move us. He uses people who just happen to show up at a specific place and time—providential circumstances orchestrated by Him and in accordance with His will and His plan. It is not *our* plan. It is His. We may not understand it, but that doesn't matter. We don't have to.

"'For I know the plans I have for you,' declares the Lord, 'plans to prosper you and not to harm you, plans to give you hope and a future'" (Jeremiah 29:11).

"At one time we too were foolish, disobedient, deceived and enslaved by all kinds of passions and pleasures. We lived in malice and envy, being hated and hating one another. But when the kindness and love of God are Savior appeared, he saved us" (Titus 3:3–5).

One night Drew awoke and as he groped his way in the dark to the kitchen, a sudden burst of dizziness drove him to his knees. He begged for help from the God he remembered from his youth.

The entrance to his tent burst open. God took control.

※

When the flap came open, Stevie reacted quickly. He hurled the rock but missed his intended target. It smacked the canvas close to where someone's head should have been and landed on the wooden floor with a thud.

"I missed! Smack him, Drew!" Stevie yelled.

Drew hesitated a second. Good thing he did.

A raspy and all-too-familiar voice blurted out, "*Hold it*! Stop! It's me!"

"Uh-oh," Stevie said. He realized whom he'd almost clobbered.

The intruder turned out to be old Mr. Michaels. He cautiously came into the tent wet and bent over to protect himself. His arm covered his head in case someone threw something else.

After the boys calmed down, he straightened and removed his hat. Water from the brim dripped onto the floor. He tossed a wet metal canteen cup onto Stevie's bunk.

"Your friends placed that by your tent earlier tonight. They put it in a spot directly under a limb where the rain was dripping. They must have figured the noise would keep you awake and worried all night. But no need to fret anymore. They're not gonna bother you tonight. They're in bed asleep."

How does he know? Drew asked himself. Regardless, a feeling of relief settled inside the tent.

Mr. Michaels looked at Drew. "Put on your rain gear and come with me. I want to show you something."

Drew looked over at Stevie for some sign of "it's OK to go with him." *What do you think I should do?*

Stevie was no help.

Drew watched him shrug as if to say, "You're on your own now."

Mr. Michaels waited as Drew slipped the poncho over his head

The old man turned and vanished through the tent opening. Drew followed him into the damp night. His mind raced.

What's going on? Where are we going? It's almost midnight. Is he taking me to their tent? Is he up to no good? He does magic—is he a witch or something?

Drew wasn't sure which was the scariest—waiting for the attack that never came...or this.

Chapter 7

THE CANVAS SANCTUARY

The rain had stopped. The sliver of a full moon shone through a small opening in the black clouds.

Mr. Michaels headed toward the other side of the campsite. He had the only flashlight, so Drew stayed in his shadow close behind him.

Drew stared at his back. *This is turning into one of the most bizarre nights I've ever had.*

He assumed they were going to Mr. Michaels's tent, but he wasn't sure. The old man said nothing, and Drew didn't ask. Staying quiet seemed best.

Drew's assumption was correct. Mr. Michaels approached his four-man canvas shelter and pulled back the front flap. He stepped aside and motioned Drew to go on in.

The inside was pitch black. Mr. Michaels flicked his silver Zippo lighter. Drew could smell the lighter fluid as the wick caught fire.

"Here. Hold this." Mr. Michaels handed Drew the flashlight. He lit a candle on a field table by the tent's entrance.

After a wheezing spell that almost blew out the flame, Mr. Michaels carried the candle to the back corner of the tent. Mr. Michaels slept on a real bed, not a cot. A metal single-size bunk.

Must be nice to have a mattress.

The old man sat on the edge of his bed and used the candle to light the propane lantern. The glowing mantles hummed as he adjusted their bright-yellow intensity so light filled the inside of the tent.

Mr. Michaels's tent was not much larger than the others. Years later, when he thought back on this night, Drew pictured the inside to be huge, like a castle sanctuary. His memory was obviously the result of a twelve-year-old's robust imagination.

Mr. Michaels pointed to a folded canvas stool leaning against the wall. "Grab that seat over there. Sit down here in front of me, Son."

Drew did as he was told. It felt good to finally sit down. He relaxed and gazed into the lantern's radiant mantles, still softly humming. Mesmerized, he waited for what would happen next.

Mr. Michaels reached into his inside coat pocket and removed something clenched in his fist. He opened up his hand.

In his palm lay four nickels.

"Observe closely. See these four nickels?" He arranged them in a neat stack.

Déjà vu. The day in the bookstore.

Drew almost blurted out to Mr. Michaels that he'd seen this before.

You remember, Mr. Michaels? Couple of years ago maybe? We were in a bookstore.

But he didn't say anything. Instead, he watched. Closer this time, though. He knew what came next.

Mr. Michaels continued. "You see, I have a way to double my money. Therefore, I will be a rich man very soon."

He reached again into his pocket. "Watch this."

He withdrew the same small brass cover. He placed it over the nickels and waved his hand like a wand.

"Before, I had twenty cents." He removed the cover. "Now, I have forty."

He spread out the four dimes. Then he handed the cover to Drew. "Here. You can inspect it if you like."

Drew checked it over carefully. Those nickels had to be somewhere. But they weren't. The circular cover was solid and empty.

Drew asked the same question he'd asked in the bookstore months ago. "How'd you do that, Mr. Michaels?"

Back then, Mr. Michaels had given no answer. But tonight he said, "Watch. I'll show you. Now pay close attention because you're going to do it after me."

Mr. Michaels again went through the routine. But this time he revealed the secrets of how he did it.

Drew listened attentively and followed his every move. When he saw how the magician made the nickels "appear" to turn into dimes, he was pleasantly surprised yet somewhat disappointed.

"So that's how..." He smiled. He was glad he knew the secret, but the excitement of having an unsolved mystery to ponder had vanished.

Mr. Michaels handed Drew the special apparatus that created the illusion. He coached Drew step-by-step through the routine. He forced Drew to focus on his timing and delivery. Together, they practiced over and over again until the magician said he was satisfied his newfound protégé could perform the effect with no mishaps.

After that, Mr. Michaels demanded that Drew rehearse the trick several more times with no coaching or instruction. "Practice, practice, practice," he said.

It was past midnight when Mr. Michaels finally said, "OK, that's enough for tonight. It's time for you to go back to your tent. You need to get some sleep..."

Drew was indeed tired. Why was it so important that the man kept him up late, changing nickels to dimes over and over again?

"...because I want you perform this trick tomorrow at the canteen while we're waiting to leave camp."

That answered Drew's question, and his initial thought was, *Oh no, I'm not.*

But before he said anything, Mr. Michaels continued. "I know you're nervous and you don't want to do this. Who wouldn't be nervous? But that is why you have to do it."

Mr. Michaels reached under his bunk and pulled out a book with a worn, brown-leather cover. It was about the same color as his nicotine-stained fingers. He cradled the book, rubbing his rough palm over the soft binding.

"You know, Son, I've had this Bible since I was your age," Mr. Michaels said. "It comes in handy during difficult times.

"I've been watching you"—cough—"and have noticed the problems you've been having with a few of the older kids, who I refer to as"— cough—"troublemakers in the troop."

Drew listened closely. By now he was so used to the man's frequent throat-clearing hacks and puffed cheeks that he didn't notice them anymore.

"I hate to tell you this," Mr. Michaels said, "but there's not much I can do about them. I've tried to have them removed from the troop, but the church leaders think it's better if they stay with the troop, which can be a good example for them. They may change their behavior."

He sighed. "But frankly, I haven't seen any indication that it's working. They're just as bad as they were a year ago when we let them join. So I deal with that."

Mr. Michaels continued. "We have to work through our adversities. You, like me, have to work through your problems and your fears. Fear of those bullies, or your fear of standing in front of a crowd of Scouts and magically turning nickels into dimes."

He opened his Bible and thumbed through it until he reached the verse he wanted to share with his most attentive apprentice.

"The apostle Paul, one of the early missionaries, wrote this letter to his friends who lived in the city of Corinth," he said. "Paul's friends were peaceful, God-fearing folk. But Corinth was an ancient port city, and many sailors and other riffraff passed through there. Many of the visitors were bad men, troublemakers like the ones you know here. They harassed the good people of Corinth, even persecuted them."

He looked down at his Bible. "Here's what Paul wrote to them in 2 Corinthians 4:8–9: 'We are hard pressed on every side by troubles, but not crushed and broken. We are perplexed, because we don't know why things happen as they do, but we don't give up and quit. We are hunted down, but God never abandons us. We get knocked down, but we get up again and keep going'" (LB).

He paused to let the words sink in. Then he asked Drew, "How do you suppose we can do that, Son? Get up again and keep going?"

Drew thought for a minute. "Because God is with us?"

The old man smiled. "Tomorrow, Son, you will begin to work through your fears and adversities. And God will be there, looking out for you."

He closed the Bible and told Drew to hurry back to his tent and get some sleep since dawn would arrive soon.

Drew still felt hesitant, reluctant to go through with the trick tomorrow. But just because he didn't want to do something… well, that really didn't matter anymore in the huge scheme of things.

Mr. Michaels had one last comment as Drew was leaving the tent. "Don't let me down. I'm counting on you."

Chapter 8

DREW'S FIRST SHOW AND MR. MICHAEL'S FINAL BOW

⌛

The off-key trumpet blare of reveille roused Drew from a fitful sleep. Anxious and nervous about what he would do today, he'd tossed and turned from the time he got into his bunk last night until now. He pulled the sleeping bag over his head.

Do I have to get up? I don't want to get up.

He reluctantly dragged himself out of the sleeping bag. He checked his pants pocket; the nickels-to-dimes apparatus was still where he'd left it, along with the coins he needed to perform the trick. He held it, rehearsing again in his mind the routine and his spiel. But he still couldn't shake the butterflies in his stomach.

I'll go over it again after breakfast. But wait a second. Who says I have to go to breakfast?

"Hey, Stevie. I'm not hungry, so you go on to breakfast without me."

Stevie slowly stirred in his cot, expression curious.

"When did you finally get back last night?" he asked.

"Late."

"What happened?"

"I'll tell you later."

Stevie took his time getting ready. Drew became more anxious. But he finally left, and Drew had about an hour to himself to practice.

He went through the act one last time. He placed the items

in his pocket and collapsed on the cot.

Gosh, I'm tired. I hope I can do this.

The last day of camp. The storm front had passed. The sky was blue. And the Scouts were preparing to leave.

After Stevie returned from breakfast, the tent mates started packing their personal gear. The troop's Scout leader stopped by.

"After you guys finish," he said, "grab a couple of trash bags and walk through the camp. Pick up all the litter and any loose paper."

"Yes, sir," Stevie said. He gave an exaggerated three-finger Scout salute, obviously mocking the Scout's authority.

"Real funny, mister," the Scout leader said. "So after you finish with that, grab some cleaning supplies and head over to the latrine."

"Way to go, Stevie," Drew said.

"Seriously, guys. We can't leave until the camp is spick and span. They won't let us go until they're satisfied the camp's ready for the next group of Scouts coming in this afternoon. We all need to pitch in so we can get out of here."

≍

Drew closed up his footlocker and placed it outside the tent. He and Stevie secured a couple of garbage bags from the camp's supply point.

Drew took charge of the operation.

"Stevie, you take that side, and I'll take the other."

By ten o'clock, camp cleanup was finished. Drew loaded his personal gear and helped stow the troop's equipment underneath the bus.

The boys were ready to go home, but like they say in the army, they could only "hurry up and wait." The scoutmasters went around with the camp staff, checking off the to-do list of things required to clear camp.

To pass the time, the Scouts came up with creative ways to

entertain themselves. A few threw around a baseball or football. Even a card game or two was dealt somewhere under the trees.

Drew had one more job to do. He headed over to the camp's canteen, a simple one-room structure with a concrete floor. The favorite hangout was full this morning. The windows were made of Plexiglas and covered with venetian blinds. About twenty square card tables, covered with red-and-white-checkered table cloths, were scattered about the room. A few wooden benches had been placed along the walls.

The man who ran the canteen was a crusty, retired World War II veteran. Known only as Ole Bob, he volunteered every summer to run the canteen. He sold hotdogs and hamburgers, and he provided cold bottles of Coke that cost a dime. Candy bars were a nickel.

Ole Bob was an easygoing sort. Most of the time he joked around with the boys and told funny war stories to young, eager ears. But he quickly reverted to no nonsense when any of them got too rowdy. So the boys respected him and, for the most part, stayed on their best behavior in his presence. Even the three bullies behaved when they were around Ole Bob.

Drew's muscles were tense, his body weary, when he arrived at the canteen. Plus his stomach churned when he thought about what lay ahead and what he was about to do.

The place was jam-packed with Scouts. It was SRO, standing room only.

Drew looked around.

Too many people here.

Good enough reason for him to leave. Forget about it.

Relieved, he turned to go back out the way he'd come in.

But there they were. Directly between him and the exit.

The bullies sat at a table near the door, facing him. Drew hadn't seen them when he came in. They obviously hadn't seen him either. They were talking loud as usual and cutting jokes. In the corner, watching the drama unfold, stood Mr. Michaels. He leaned against the wall, the ever-present cigarette dangling from his lips. His arms were folded. He looked relaxed, an audience of one waiting patiently for the curtain to rise.

Drew swallowed hard. He couldn't turn back now. He had nowhere to run.

I have to suck it up. Do what the old man over there watching told me to do.

The lump in his throat grew to the size of the knot in his stomach. It seemed as if the whole camp were here. As he fully recognized what he was about to do, his initial fear was now close to outright panic.

The play button on the tape recorder in his mind engaged.

All eyes are on you. What if you blow it? What happens when you mess it up? You'll be laughed at. You're a real idiot, they'll say. You'll never live it down.

The tape repeated over and over.

He looked at Mr. Michaels, his eyes pleading.

Do I have to?

Mr. Michaels motioned with his hand, a circular-like gesture that said, "Get on with it, Son."

All right already. I'm going.

A calm swept over Drew.

Why am I worried? I earned my merit badges. Camp's over. I'll be home soon. I'll never see these people again.

Adrenaline kicked in.

Let's get this over with.

Drew took a deep breath and dived in. He had the four nickels in one hand and the secret apparatus palmed in the other. He marched straight to the bullies' table. They saw him coming and stopped what they were doing.

Their eyes said it.

What's this stupid punk up to?

Two steps before he reached their table, though, Drew diverted to the left and stopped at the table next to them. He didn't know the Scouts sitting there. Had never seen them. But that was OK.

Drew had his introduction memorized, or at least he thought he did. He had rehearsed it a zillion times, but…he wasn't really sure what came out. He spoke loudly enough for everyone at the surrounding tables to hear.

"Hey, wanna see how to double your money and get real rich real quick? Check this out!"

He opened his hand in front of the closest Scout, a skinny, goofy-looking kid with Coke-bottle glasses and buck teeth.

The room became quiet.

The silence and stares said it all.

Who is this guy? Get rich? What's this all about?

Drew glanced over at the bullies' table and for just a second made direct eye contact with the leader. Rob stared at him with a what-the-heck-do-you-think-you're-doing? look on his face. He didn't look happy.

Good. He had their attention.

And that's all he wanted.

Drew went through his patter and routine without a hitch. But as he was placing the brass cover over the stack of nickels, one of the bullies said, "The guy's crazy. He can't do nuthin'."

"He's messing with you guys," one of the other bullies said. "Watch out! He's going to try and steal something."

Drew waved his hand over the cover and chanted the first thing that came to mind. "Hocus-pocus! Abracadabra!"

He lifted the cover.

Four dimes.

I did it. It worked.

The goofy kid stared at the coins. He removed his thick glasses and lowered his head close enough so his nose almost touched the dimes.

"Wow," he whispered. Followed by the usual question. "How'd you do that?"

Drew smiled and shrugged.

"Yeah, how did you do that?" a Scout from an adjacent table asked.

"How'd you do that?" another Scout asked.

"You gotta show me, man!"

"Are you Houdini or something?"

Scouts crowded in for a closer look.

Amid the commotion, another idea leaped into Drew's mind out of nowhere. He announced to the spectators around him, "You know what else I can do? I can read minds, too."

Drew turned and faced the three bullies. "Here's one for you."

To appear in deep concentration, he closed his eyes and brought his hand up to his forehead. "Bee. Oh. See," he chanted, accentuating each word. He opened his eyes, pointed at them, and exclaimed, "B. O. C. means 'bridge over creek'!"

The three looked at each other in surprise. And that was that.

Drew turned back to the cluster of boys, who wanted some insight into how he had really doubled the money. They had no idea what "bridge over creek" meant. That didn't matter to Drew. The ones who knew got the message.

In spite of the attempted disruption and flawed attempt to bring attention back to them, the bullies were now ignored. They had been dethroned from their once-feared position as the bad boys of camp. They slinked out the front door, possibly to wait by themselves for the buses to begin loading.

※

The boys crowded around Drew, hoping for an answer. Mr. Michaels smiled, satisfied with how the effect had turned out. Quietly and unnoticed, he slipped out through a side door.

He limped to the wood line; the week's activities had taken a toll on his worn-out knee. He stopped at a clump of soft moss under an oak tree and sat down.

He looked up through the green tree branches and admired the deep blue sky. *God's handiwork.*

As he often did at times like this, he talked with his Father.

Young Drew did pretty good today, don't You think? He certainly surprised me a couple of times…Yes sir, I'm sure You had

THE MAGIC OF GRACE

something to do with that. You know, I was ready to jump in there at the start when they were giving him a hard time. But thanks to You, I didn't have to.

And shifting over to the other table? That was perfect. Kept the spotlight off the bad guys, but they got what they needed just the same. A little humility was just the ticket.

But "bridge over creek"!

He laughed out loud and coughed.

That was beautiful.

"I can read minds, too," he said, still chuckling.

One day he'll realize he didn't read any minds that day. He'll know where the thought really came from.

Well, the boys should be boarding about now. Guess I should see them off.

But before I go, just one more thing. Please watch over young Drew. There's something special about him. He still has a full life in front of him. And like the rest of us, he'll have good times, but he'll have some tough periods, too. He'll need You during those times. Even though he won't realize it. He'll need Your protection. Just like I did.

Thank You, Father. For allowing me to share these boys' lives for a short time.

As You know, this'll be my last camp. But I know You have more for me to do. More boys are out there who need a little magic in their lives.

The magic of Your grace.

⋻⋵

The boys raved about Drew's trick during the entire bus ride home. They figured he didn't actually change the coins, but they were curious about how he'd made it look like he did.

Drew made many new friends that day. And, to his surprise, even Rob, the leader of the gang who had made his week miserable, came up to him as the bus pulled into the church parking lot.

"That was pretty good, kid," Rob said. "You're OK. Sorry about taking your clothes. Glad you found them." He reached out his hand.

Drew looked at his hand for a moment, then shook it.

"No hard feelings, right?" Rob said.

"No," Drew said. "See ya around."

Drew got off the bus. His dad was standing by the car, waiting. Drew waved and hurried to grab his gear.

He stopped.

Where's Mr. Michaels? I need to say good-bye. And say thank you.

He looked around.

The old man was nowhere to be seen.

Drew was puzzled.

I thought he was coming back with us. I remember seeing him back at the parking lot, watching us get on the bus. But wait a second...he was waving. Was that good-bye? Maybe so.

Drew shook his head.

Oh, well. I'm really gonna miss him, though.

Drew headed over to the car, eager to tell his Dad about his week. All in all, it had been a good one. And he didn't think his dad would be displeased this time.

⋈

It wasn't until two years later that Drew was able to thank the old man and say his final good-bye. Ironically, their last encounter happened at the same place where they'd first met—the bookstore.

Since then, Drew's reading preference had changed from comic books to paperbacks. He was browsing through the mystery novels when the front door opened. Sunlight penetrated the musty room.

Drew looked up. There stood Mr. Michaels.

The man gazed around, apparently looking for someone. Anyone, maybe. Drew's first thought was how much older the man looked. Some things, however, hadn't changed. Mr. Michaels wore the same coat and hat, and a lit cigarette dangled from his brown lips. He grabbed it and pulled it out of his mouth.

He coughed. Coughed again. The spasms were more intense than they'd been before. He wheezed, wiped the spittle off his mouth with the back of a hand, and looked straight at Drew.

"Good mornin', Son."

The vacant stare told Drew that the old man didn't recognize him. Mr. Michaels glanced down at his open hand. "You ever seen this?"

Drew looked down. Four nickels rested on his palm.

A flood of memories from two summers ago rushed back. Drew looked into the sick man's yellow, bloodshot eyes.

What do I say?

He thought for a second.

Well, that's easy.

"No, sir."

And once again, Mr. Michaels did his magic.

This time Drew didn't ask the normal question. He just said, "Wow! That was amazing. Thank you, sir."

Mr. Michaels smiled. He wheezed again and turned to leave.

But before he could get out the door, Drew said, "Hey, Mr. Michaels!"

The old man stopped. He slowly turned and looked back at Drew.

"Thank you, Mr. Michaels. For everything."

Mr. Michaels looked puzzled. He cocked his head slightly. Drew could only surmise what he was thinking.

Wonder how he knows my name.

And once again the old man smiled. He turned and was gone, his coattail flapping behind him as a strong breeze met him at the door.

EPILOGUE

⋈

Drew gazed into the slowly dying bonfire, still clutching the bag carrying his pretend rabbit.

He never forgot the old scoutmaster. Years after their last encounter, Drew was curious to know whatever happened to him. After a number of phone calls to people from his hometown, he discovered that Mr. Michaels had passed away shortly after that day at the bookstore when he last saw him. He now rests at the local VA cemetery.

Drew's gaze followed the sparks as the floated up into the starry sky. He thought back over the years of his adult life. And he prayed:

Thank you, Father. Thank you for all you did to bring me to where I am tonight. Thank you for your mercy and your grace, especially for looking out for me and caring about me. You were always there, Lord, even when I didn't realize it. And thank you for Mr. Michael's—for bringing him into my life and for what he showed me.

When Drew first taught Sunday school, he discovered that magic made an excellent teaching venue for youngsters. He remembered his first class. He talked about how God can change people. He used magic to illustrate the point. Guess which trick he used first?

Every week the kids looked forward to see what new effect Mr. Seward came up with. His repertoire grew.

Drew's prayer was suddenly interrupted.

"Hey, Mr. Seward!"

It was Bobby.

"Can I play with Herby? Please. Please. Where is Herby?"

Drew chuckled. Bobby's dad was Drew's friend, Rob. The same Rob who had taken his clothes at camp years ago. They were pretty close now and had been for some time. So were their sons. They attended Sunday school together.

Well, I guess it won't hurt to violate rule number one this time.

Drew tossed the bag to Bobby. "Catch. And go find Danny. He can show you how to play with Herby."

Bobby dashed away, holding out the bag. A few seconds later, a high-pitched, excited voice echoed in the distance.

"I knew it wasn't real! Hey, guys! Look at Herby!"

Oh, well. I'm sure Mr. Michaels understands.

The evening festivities came to a close. The flame of the bonfire started to die down. By morning, the pit would be full of charred wood and ash. Taps started to play. Everyone was still.

Although today was done and the sun was gone, God was still nigh. And He was not finished with the teacher-magician yet.